In 1785, Vienna's gaiety has been curbed by the Emperor who has closed all public amusements. The nobility, led by the elegant Count Anton von Arnheim, refuse to have their pleasures curtailed. The Count's home is called the House of Satan, for the gambling, dancing and flirtation so beloved by the Viennese continues there undisturbed. And into this notorious mansion comes Eloise, his innocently beautiful ward.

How can so unscrupulous a rake become the guardian of such a young and unworldly girl? And how can the spirited Eloise, thrilled to be introduced to the sophisticated pursuits of the Count, go on living in the House of Satan with the man who threatens to own her body and soul?

House of Satan

Gina Veronese

MILLS & BOON LIMITED
London · Sydney · Toronto

First published in Great Britain 1980
by Mills & Boon Limited, 15–16 Brook's Mews,
London W1

© Gina Veronese 1980

Australian copyright 1980
Philippine copyright 1980
ISBN 0 263 73231 2

Set in Times 11 on 12pt

Made and printed in Great Britain by
C. Nicholls & Company Ltd.,
The Philips Park Press, Manchester

CHAPTER
ONE

ELOISE felt stifling. The air inside the carriage was close and stuffy, since Aunt Maria had insisted that the blinds be drawn as soon as dusk fell, shutting out the glorious spring evening outside. Suddenly the girl could stand it no longer: the lurching rumble of wheels drumming through her head as they crossed the high Semmering Pass and descended to the plains leading to Vienna, the silent, shadowy figure of her aunt in the opposite corner, huddling crossly into her thick, black pelisse and bonnet as if it were midwinter instead of April.

'Please, Aunt Maria—oh, *please* let us stop and pass the night at an inn,' she cried in desperation. 'The hour must be very late by now and Vienna still many leagues ahead.'

'You are as selfish as your late father,' her aunt replied tartly, adding hastily, 'though one mustn't speak ill of the dead. No, I insist on reaching my own little home tonight, and dear Gertrude who, alone in all the world, understands how frail—indeed, how *dangerously* frail I am, although I never complain!'

The voice grew querulous as she thought longingly of her faithful servant, who would fuss round her with apfelstrudel, mulled wine and a soft bed-shawl while listening with clucking sympathy to the tales of suffering and discomfort her poor, dear Frau Maria had endured so nobly in dutifully fetching her orphaned niece all the way from Carinthia, in Southern Austria, to Vienna. 'One more night in a draughty inn and a damp bed and *I* shall die,' she finished, quite over-come with self-pity.

Eloise was too angry to trust her voice immediately, thinking of the robust, rosy-cheeked aunt who had arrived at the small château above the Wörther See two days ago—conveniently too late for the funeral of her only brother, but bursting with disapproval at the plans he had made for his daughter in his will. Since Eloise was barely eighteen and a minor it had not been thought seemly for her to hear the will in person. Besides, the elderly lawyer did not fancy the long journey from Vienna to Carinthia to collect a mere child, so he had read it to her aunt instead, assuring her that he would find enough money from her brother's estate to hire a carriage to take her on this mission.

So, during a delicious meal of roast venison followed by rich apricot dumplings, of which Aunt Maria ate six, she told Eloise what the future held.

'Your dear father knew quite well how poor I am,' she began, glancing meaningly round the small but well-furnished dining-room, 'so my humble abode in Hietzing would be no fit place from which to launch you into Viennese society. Instead he has appointed Count Anton von Arnheim as your guardian—a wealthy man who came to him for some special tuition many years ago, and whom he has never set eyes on since.' She pursed her lips, moist with apricot sauce. 'A *very* strange choice, so it seems to a woman of the world like myself—but there, scholars like Franz are often foolish in such matters and at least you will want for nothing. For you are poor now, too, Eloise,' her eyes sparked with malice. 'The lawyer tells me this place must be sold at once to provide you with a small allowance and, we hope, a dowry!'

Questions were racing through her mind but, for a moment, Eloise stared out of the window to the still waters of the Wörther See that mirrored every tree along the shore. Her eyes were wide, the deep blue of gentians fringed with long black lashes, and her spine was tingling at the thought of Vienna—society—life in a wealthy household.

She grieved deeply for her father, for their relationship had been very close indeed. He had not only tried to make up for her mother who had died at her birth, but educated Eloise himself to an unusually high standard for a girl in 1785. Yet of late she had been restless, wandering alone through the pine forests or along the lake shore, lost in romantic dreams and a sense that life must surely hold much, much more than she would find in this quiet place. Every local swain had laid his heart at the feet of her undoubted beauty—but they could not talk with her of books and foreign lands; also she could out-climb them all in the mountains, which did not breed respect on that level either. So she had waited, often impatiently, for she knew not what.

Now it had come—at the cost of her dear father's life—but the very name Vienna held a potent magic, and the hint that her unknown guardian was unsuitable merely increased the excitement.

'Aunt Maria, *why* do you not find Count Anton a wise choice? My father was rarely wrong about people.'

The elderly widow helped herself to her fifth

dumpling and, forgetting her niece's tender age, launched into the gossip so dear to her heart. In fact the best time during her days at home was when four dear friends—all lonely and a trifle bitter—sat around in her small *salle*, enjoying mocha frothed with cream and slices of rich chocolate törte to exchange, with embellishments, the rumours of the city.

'Of course,' she began comfortably, 'my little house is only in the suburbs of Vienna, but news travels fast and you may as well know soon as late, that your guardian has earned the title of "Count Satan", Eloise. Goodness, the Emperor Josef would run mad if he knew half the goings-on in rich houses! And now I am to escort you into the most infamous of all—home of the very Devil incarnate!'

She spooned more thick cream over her dumpling as Eloise said levelly, not wanting to stop the flow: 'There are goings-on, as you call them, here in the country too.'

'Ah! But not like his, you poor innocent lamb. What do you know of gambling—of a man who trifles with women so cruelly that it is said two Princesses from France and Germany, as well as half the great beauties in Vienna itself, have almost died of broken hearts?'

'How stupid they must be!' Eloise exclaimed impulsively. 'Why, in our village if Herr Schreiber starts to flirt with a girl, she laughs in his face! Everyone knows he does not mean it!'

Her aunt stared at her with dislike—a feeling that had been growing steadily ever since her arrival, although she would never admit that it was jealousy. Eloise had all the attributes she lacked and would, inevitably, be a success in society. Mentally she dismissed her as 'a pretty little thing', firmly refusing the deeper knowledge that her niece was not only a great beauty but blessed with brains.

This sourness stemmed from the time, many years ago, when Franz Reisdorf had implored his sister Maria to join him in Carinthia as his companion and housekeeper, since he was so taken up with his studies that he did not expect to marry. Then a spinster of twenty-two, she had scorned the offer, feeling that her chances lay in Vienna, for she was determined to gain a husband. She did, only to find herself tied to a drunken baker who soon collapsed in the heat of his bakery, leaving her childless, poor, with only the small villa in Hietzing to show for her decision. Meantime, her brother Franz had married a beautiful girl from the Tyrol who had brought a fine dowry, managed his house to perfection and given him four years of great happiness before she died in childbirth. Because she could not forgive herself, Maria never forgave him either. Her resentment grew steadily as she looked at his daughter.

'Then perhaps,' she said caustically, 'you will be a match for this Count of yours. Since you seem to have no modesty, I suppose you will either take to bad ways yourself or reform the man.'

'Has he no wife?' asked Eloise, wisely ignoring the suggestion.

Aunt Maria cast pious eyes to the ceiling, while considering whether she had room for just one more of the delicious dumplings.

'Praise be, no woman has had to undergo such an indignity.'

She took the dumpling, since Eloise had turned to stare out of the window again, planning just how she would present herself to this elderly roué. She had few clothes, as country life did not demand high fashion, but for her eighteenth birthday three months ago, her father had ordered the village dressmaker, Frau Schmidt, to make her a dress from a roll of exquisite lilac silk stored in her mother's closet, and to trim it he had bought lace from a pedlar. The result was magnificent.

'It is the very latest style, Eloise,' Frau Schmidt had assured her, scarlet with pride. 'A fine lady rested the night at our Hotel Post not long ago, and I observed her gown most carefully. See—you have the new ruffled lace bodice edged with velvet ribbon—and ruffles at the neck and elbows, too! I declare it suits you so well that it makes your eyes seem violet rather than dark blue!'

It was true, and Eloise had determined that she would wear it to meet her unknown guardian. He must be quite an old man now, if her father had not seen him for so long, so he would treat her as a daughter. But she must be a witty and amusing one, so that he would take pride in presenting her at Court and even hold balls and soirées for her where she could meet young people. If she bored him he might not bother, and such loneliness was unthinkable. But already she half loved the stately, elegant figure forming in her mind. His behaviour in public might shock women like Aunt Maria, but her father had known the real man, otherwise he would never have chosen him out of all Austria to care for her future....

Because the hired carriage would cost more the longer the driver waited, packing had been done in a feverish rush, leaving Eloise little or no time to feel sad at leaving her home. Besides, she thought, she would often be back to see all her friends and the faithful servants who had helped to bring her up.

'I shall have some money of my own—and my guardian is very rich,' she had told them all eagerly. 'I shall come home often to visit you I promise—so this is not goodbye. Why, Count Anton may even let me invite friends to stay with us in Vienna!'

She had told no one, not even her closest friend Trudi, that he was known as 'Satan'—with her fiercely independent spirit she had preferred to wait and make her own judgement when she knew him.

The lilac silk gown was folded carefully in swathes of butter muslin at the top of her large valise, ready to be put on at the very last stop of the journey. She hoped it would be only an hour or two before they reached Vienna. With it she would wear her mother's gold locket on a velvet ribbon and, even if the spring weather proved a little chilly, just a fine, hand-woven white shawl round her shoulders. Oh, she could picture her arrival so vividly! Bewigged and powdered footmen in satin knee-breeches to open the wide doors into Count Anton's mansion—and then the man himself, tall and grey-haired like her father, in rich silks and lace ruffles with, perhaps, a quizzing-glass to see her better as he leant on a gold-topped ebony cane....

Now, imprisoned in the loathsome carriage, Aunt Maria had torn that dream apart. Eloise was to be delivered at dead of night like some shameful parcel, tired, travel-stained and dressed in the hideous black alpaca that Frau Schmidt had run up hastily for her mourning. Frantically, she made one final appeal.

'If you must reach your own house—may I not spend the night there with you?' In spite of herself, Eloise's voice broke. 'Surely noon will be a more seemly time for me to arrive? And even your Satan will not appear too wicked at midday!'

It failed.

'There is scarce room for Gertrude and myself in Hietzing,' snapped her aunt, woken from a welcome doze. 'Believe me, child, you will fare much better if you are taken in by servants. Then you can avoid the Count for as long as possible. Really,' she went on plaintively, 'you seem to have no gratitude whatever—no thought at all for what your poor aunt has undergone in taking this wearisome journey twice within a week, entirely for your benefit.'

With stormy tears of defiance in her eyes Eloise said nothing, but deliberately pushed up the blind so that she could at least see the clear, starlit sky and breathe more freely. She knew quite well that her aunt had passed two nights at comfortable inns on her way to Carinthia—now they had passed only one, and the old woman seemed determined to ruin the start of her niece's grand new life.

But it was a challenge, and as she thought of it like that, the tears dried and her small, firm chin rose determinedly to meet it. People were so quickly dazzled by Eloise's great dark eyes and flower-like face they seldom noticed that chin, which was a grave mistake for, small and slender as she was, Eloise was a born fighter. It was that quality which had forced her to overcome an early terror of heights until she could climb like a chamois—ignoring her nurse's wailing cry of, 'Not so high, Liebchen—not so *high* or you will surely fall!'

And she would not be defeated now. She, Eloise Reisdorf, daughter of a famous if impoverished scholar, would enter her guardian's house with as

much pride at midnight as at midday, wearing the drab
mourning garments as the armour of respectability.

In the early hours of the morning the House of Satan,
as it had been jokingly dubbed by his friends, was still
ablaze with light. A large, grey stone mansion, it stood
in the fashionable Josefstrasse, the massive double
front doors emblazoned with the coat of arms of the
von Arnheim family. Along the entire length of the
first floor crystal chandeliers shone brilliantly, bearing
a thousand candles apiece, and the dividing doors
between the reception rooms were flung open so that
Count Anton's guests could wander at will between
the gambling tables, the ballroom and the more discreetly lit supper room where shaded candles on small
tables gave an illusion of privacy to amorous couples.

The stern, reforming Emperor Josef II had closed
all public places of amusement in an effort to restrain
and re-educate his gaiety-loving people. But rich
young nobles would have none of it—instead revelry
was the rule in one house or another, night after night,
where swaggering blades and beautiful women
danced, flirted and gambled the hours away, often to
excess. And, since Count Anton was the acknowledged leader of society, his parties were the most
popular of all.

But tonight he held aloof, his mood out of tune with
the general laughter—further loosened by wine proffered regularly in each room by footmen. To add
to his ill-humour the most notorious—though unproved—cheat in Vienna, Gerhard von Eckerman,
was surrounded by a bevy of young women in the
ballroom as he tried to teach them the latest waltz
steps. He had won enough at the gaming tables to

cover his immediate needs and felt free to exert his considerable charm which, among women, was second only to that of Count Anton himself. He was never actually invited to these gatherings, but contrived to arrive as escort to some currently favourite beauty, so that he could not reasonably be turned away.

Anton's eyes smouldered as he watched the man cavorting on the dance floor from his own vantage point at a quiet table in the supper room where he sat alone. But the source of his anger went much deeper. How dared his almost forgotten tutor, Franz Reisdorf, presume to bequeath him a ward—some chit named Eloise who, subject to the sale of a small château above the Wörther See, should cause him no financial embarrassment, the nervous lawyer had assured him. *Embarrassment!* Mere money mattered not at all—but the infliction of a young girl into his house and—worse still—his care, was unthinkable.

Anton von Arnheim was not only the most eligible but the most confirmed bachelor in Vienna, and intended to remain so. He adored women for what they were in a moment of desire, but had no use for them as a permanent factor in his life. The name 'Satan', conferred for his seemingly heartless treatment of women, caused him much cynical amusement. For he knew, perfectly well, that the women he dallied with—much more rarely than gossip reported—were quite as heartless as he. They were clever schemers, the lot of them, wanting only to become châtelaine over the house in Josefstrasse—with a handsome settlement from the von Arnheim fortune, naturally—so that they could crow over their unsuccessful rivals.

For a moment his eyes grew bleak, forcing back a memory that, even now, was unendurable. At that instant his current mistress, the widowed Carla von Schernberg, slid into the vacant chair opposite to him. She was pretty in the style of the new Dresden pottery figures just making an appearance in rich Viennese houses, her round blue eyes sparkling and a bewitching smile curving her small pink mouth.

'Anton, do not look so serious I pray.' She tapped his arm coquettishly with her fan. 'You are brooding over this wretched Reisdorf girl from the country, I can tell—but I have told you, I shall arrange *everything*. She is still but a child and I will engage a governess and a maid when she arrives, then pouf! You can banish her to your deserted East Wing where you need never set eyes on her at all....'

'She most certainly will *not* occupy the East Wing,' replied Anton tersely.

'Oh come, my love,' Carla's tinkling laugh obviously annoyed her lover but, like some of her predecessors, she was consumed with curiosity about that East Wing which remained permanently closed. 'Surely it is the ideal place for her? There she will not hear our laughter in the evenings, nor guess at our intimate life in your private suite. By the way, have you ever told me how she has become your ward? I forget.'

Anton looked across at her with distaste, and the coldness in his eyes made her tremble. Had she presumed too far? But he spoke evenly.

'I have not told you—but there is no secret about it. Reisdorf was once my tutor and held great belief in my future as a scholar.' His mouth curled sardonically. 'So much so that he saved my life, I recollect, when I developed cramp while swimming. Well, I owe him no gratitude for that now—better I had died with my youthful illusions intact.'

'Oh, Anton, what nonsense! You have Vienna at your feet—and surely *my* love has not proved a disillusionment?' She pouted a little, waiting for a passionate denial—a swift apology.

Neither came. Instead, Anton looked at her with the detachment of a complete stranger. How on earth had he tolerated such shallow insincerity during the past week? His laugh was light and cutting as he stood up.

'My dear Carla, your accomplishments as a mistress are charming, but never make the mistake of confusing them with love!'

He strolled away to the gaming tables, leaving her furious and frustrated—so much so that one of the ivory sticks of her fan snapped unnoticed in her tight grasp. She had been virtually dismissed—and how unfortunate that she had recently felt so secure in his favour she had begun boasting amongst her friends, hinting that soon she would be the undisputed hostess at the great house in Josefstrasse.

Oh, it was too provoking! And refusing to admit that she might be to blame for her failure, she promptly decided that the fault lay with Eloise Reisdorf—Anton had not been in good humour since the news of her imminent arrival. Well, Carla decided, her blue eyes chilling to marble, when the creature *did* arrive she should have no help from her!

At that moment the carriage bringing Eloise to her new home was already in Vienna. With rapt attention she stared out at the dark streets, the buildings seeming to tower up against the spring sky. Here and there a light showed or a carriage with lanterns lit on each side passed them by. It was mysterious and thrilling—like the presents piled in her small shoes on the Eve of St Nicholas when she was a child, waiting to be explored when dawn came, and meanwhile only to be guessed at.

Aunt Maria was looking out too, delighted and thankful to be so near her home at last. But when Eloise asked, with a touch of nervousness, 'You will come in while I meet Count Anton, won't you?' The reply was sharp.

'Enter *that* man's door? Never!' Although Maria was to regret this next day when her cronies came round at an unheard-of early hour, avid for news of what the splendid, infamous mansion was like inside and, above all, a description of Count Satan himself, since no one in their circle had ever seen him.

Eloise gave a little sigh, then decided that after all, it might be better—and far more dramatic—if she arrived alone. Although, as the carriage turned into Josefstrasse and slowed down before the tall, lighted windows she felt a final tremor of misgiving—her ugly black dress could have been explained easily to her elderly guardian, but as a sudden burst of laughter floated out, she wondered if she could carry it off if a big ball were in progress, thronged with fashionable people.

The carriage stopped, and with a cool 'I wish you goodbye, Aunt Maria and—thank you,' Eloise stepped out and asked the driver to bring down her two valises from the top. His manner was surly—he, too, had expected another free night at an inn and meant to charge the old woman inside an exorbitant sum for the prolonged hours of driving. But Eloise ignored the rude way in which he dumped down her bags by the great doors—she had had a brilliant idea. She would ask the footmen who answered her knock, to show her instantly to her room, so that she could change before making a first appearance.

It never occurred to her that she might not be expected for some days yet. But there was no welcome on the face of the elderly butler in dark green and gold livery who cautiously opened half the double door and stared at her.

'I am Fraulein Reisdorf—Count Anton von Arnheim will be expecting me,' Eloise said firmly as the carriage, bearing Aunt Maria to her house, clattered away into the distance.

'The Master has left no instructions,' he said doubtfully, then an unpleasant, knowing look came into his small eyes. 'Or are you to be shown straight up to his private suite?' At which point he caught sight of her luggage and his eyebrows shot up. 'Though young ladies here for *that* purpose never come prepared for a prolonged stay!'

Eloise tired, hungry and suddenly very much alone, flew into a rage. How *dared* this man assume she was a harlot? Drawing herself up to her full five feet three inches she said imperiously: 'Kindly escort me to *my* room, and have my valises brought up so that I may change into more suitable attire to meet my guardian!'

The man's face crumpled with dismay. He knew, as did all the servants, that some country girl was to be foisted on the household before very long, but no preparations for her had been either ordered or made. And if she reported his reception of her to the Count he would certainly be dismissed. He cringed as he tried to repair the blunder, urging her to step inside with much fulsome bowing and nervous smiles.

He picked up both her heavy bags himself and placed them in the big, marbled hall, instead of calling for a flunkey. 'Alas, Fräulein, we have had no instructions as to your arrival ... though, indeed, I do *welcome* you to the House of Arnheim ... oh, yes, you are *very* welcome. But I cannot escort you to a room, since I do not know which one the Count has assigned to your use. Excuse me, I will tell him you are here.' And, leaving her standing in the hall, he scuttled up the wide, curving staircase.

To calm herself, Eloise looked around her. Her dream-picture of a courtly, grey-haired man coming through one of the many doors round the hall to receive her melted away. Obviously he was still living up to his reputation as Satan, regardless of advanced years—and the house itself had a chilling atmosphere, in spite of the tall, square, wood-packed stove which glowed cheerfully, its earthenware tiles shining.

Everywhere showed evidence of riches—tapestried walls, gilt lions rampant on the newel-posts of the staircase and a handsome chandelier hanging from the ceiling on four gilt chains from which half-burnt-out candles were dripping a little grease on the floor below, because of the late hour and the fact that many young footmen had succumbed to wine and left their duties to sleep.

The old butler came down even more urgently than he had gone up.

'Oh, Fräulein, I am sorry, but the Master wants you to join the company straight away. May I take your coat and bonnet first?'

He fussed round her with real concern as she

divested herself thankfully of the old-fashioned black bonnet and grey dust-coat borrowed from Frau Schmidt for the journey, since she usually went bare-headed in the country, and possessed no travelling coat suitable for mourning. He laid them across a carved chair, then bowed to her yet again.

'This way, Fräulein, if you please.'

The sound of revelry increased as she neared the top of the stairs—a vast sea of voices surging closer and closer to engulf her so that she paused for a moment, suddenly longing to run away. Then, holding her small head high, she signalled to the butler that he should announce her.

As her name rang out above the clamour it ceased abruptly. Only the rustle of rich silk as women crowded forward to see her greeted Eloise when she stood, a tiny dark figure, framed by the white and gold doors of the ballroom. Then her glance flew straight to a tall, slender man who was moving slowly to meet her and she gave a little gasp. *This* couldn't be her guardian, surely?

He looked scarce more than thirty and was the handsomest creature she had ever seen, with dark eyes set wide above high cheekbones, a long, sensitive mouth and thick black hair drawn back into a velvet bow on the nape of his neck above the brocade collar of his coat.

He so riveted her attention that she forgot the hundred or more other people staring at her. There was no welcome in his sombre eyes, no smile touched his lips. Yet absurdly, instead of being discountenanced by this coolness, Eloise felt he had the saddest face she had ever seen, and the fact intrigued her more, even, than finding him young and handsome.

On his side, Anton was not aware of his stern expression. He was too shocked by the appearance of what might well have been a ghost in his doorway, the likeness was so uncanny. He saw a small, proud girl of exceptional beauty, enhanced rather than diminished by her plain black dress. The enormous violet-blue eyes held the intelligent directness he had long ceased to expect in a woman, while her delicate, heart-shaped face was framed by a cloud of soft, black hair that had never known the attentions of a fashionable hairdresser, but gleamed with natural highlights which made him momentarily ache to reach out and touch its silkiness.

She wore no powder or patches, no artificial rouge or aids to beauty, which in his view reduced all the exquisitely dressed, painted and coiffed women in the room to the status of mere dolls. Eloise might be his ward—but she was also danger! Forcing a smile to his lips, Count Anton went up to her, raised her hand and kissed it.

'Fräulein Reisdorf, convention decrees that one should not kiss the hand of an unmarried woman, but since you are my ward I do it to assure you of my welcome!'

His voice was deep and sincere. Eloise smiled, looking down at his dark, bowed head. 'Thank you, Count Anton,' she said, 'and I must apologise for arriving at such an unconventional hour! My aunt was determined to return to her home as soon as possible, otherwise I would have presented myself here at noon—far more suitably dressed for such an occasion, I assure you.'

When he raised his head Anton towered above her, and he had fully regained his normal tight control over his emotions. All trace of inward sadness had vanished; instead, like a cool, smiling statue, he offered her his arm to lead her forward amongst his guests. But Eloise felt a curious sensation of loss—as though she had briefly glimpsed a man she might have grown to know and love, who had turned into a complete stranger. Which of course he was, she reminded herself sharply.

She had no idea that the hour was almost three o'clock in the morning, so that it must be six hours at least since she had last eaten anything during her exhausting journey—and then only a brioche and coffee. Therefore she was surprised to find the brilliant figures swaying and blurring a little before her eyes as the Count gravely introduced her to one group after another. Suddenly a tall, dark girl caught her hand and looked up reprovingly at Anton.

'You are a monster!' she teased. 'Poor Fräulein Reisdorf has been travelling all day and you are too busy showing her off like one of your prize ponies to remember that she may need food and wine! You come with me, my dear, before you swoon—I do declare you have gone white as paper.'

Gratefully, Eloise smiled back and meekly allowed herself to be led into the supper room. Wide awake now from curiosity to see the Count's ward, eager young footmen sprang to serve her with fine hock from the Arnheim vineyards and a delicious dish of salmon mousse, thick with cream under the aspic, then tender slices of veal cooked in a rich sauce. Too dizzy with hunger to feel ashamed, Eloise ate the mousse voraciously then, as colour returned to her cheeks and the scene steadied, she smiled gratefully at her kind companion.

'Forgive me—and thank you,' she said. 'I have never swooned in my whole life, but I do believe you were right and I must have been starving! What is your name?'

'Serafina—and I hope we shall become friends.'

'I hope so too. I shall need much advice and guidance here, I can see!' Indeed, now that she felt restored, Eloise gazed wide-eyed at the elegant figures beginning to hover round the table, smiling and yet assessing her at the same time. Her poor, treasured lilac silk faded to frumpishness compared to the rich brocades and embroidered satins of the women, and the brilliance of their jewels quite took her breath away. Several wore the new small crinoline which emphasised a tiny waist most charmingly, and when she noticed the careful loops and intricate ringlets in which their hair was dressed, Eloise felt self-conscious about her own.

She was so busy trying to assimilate so much all at once that she failed to notice the frank admiration with which the young men stared at her—but it did not go unnoticed by the women, especially Carla von Schernberg, who was fuming at the way things were turning out. This was no young chit to be tucked away with a governess out of sight, but a beauty and, worse, a rival. In a clear, brittle voice she asked: 'Pray, how old are you my dear Eloise? We have been dying for your arrival, I swear, and quite expected a child. But perhaps you are, after all?'

Eloise met her hostile gaze, thinly veiled by a smile, with level eyes. 'I fear I must disappoint you, my lady, I am eighteen and quite grown up.'

Several people tittered at the cool young voice, so free from guile, that clearly expressed the girl's dislike of the popular young Countess. She was brave, but foolish to make such a dangerous enemy within an hour of her arrival. But Eloise had no experience of the bitter jealousies and cruel tongues that ran rife in smart circles.

To make matters worse, she now turned back to Serafina and said eagerly: 'If you will really be my friend, perhaps you will be kind enough to help me in the matter of my wardrobe tomorrow? I'm afraid my country clothes are quite unsuitable here, and I am so anxious that Count Anton should not feel ashamed of me!'

Carla laughed. 'You need not worry on *that* score, my child—Anton loves any novel attraction! Such a pity that he so soon grows bored with it!'

'I shall be delighted to help you,' Serafina's warm voice chipped in hastily. 'I will call on you without fail tomorrow.'

And Gerhard von Eckerman, whose eyes had been devouring Eloise ardently ever since her first appearance, seized his chance to soften Carla's words. Introducing himself with a bow, he said, 'Your beauty has so dazzled us already, Fräulein, that I must put in my humble plea to be allowed to escort you sometimes, before every eligible man in Vienna is waiting hopefully at your door! I trust you will grant me that honour?'

Eloise looked up at the pleading blue eyes, and her face glowed with shy gratitude.

'How very kind of you—I shall be delighted.' Then she suddenly remembered that she was a ward and added, smiling, 'As long as my guardian permits it, of course.'

Count Anton arrived on the scene in time to overhear this exchange, and his cold look forced von Eckerman to take a step back from his attentive place beside Eloise's chair.

'You presume too much too soon, von Eckerman,' the Count said firmly. 'My ward has only just entered my house, and no plans for her social activities will be made as yet. Come, Eloise, I have had my house-keeper wakened and a room prepared for you—you must be in need of sleep.'

It was true—and yet she was loth to leave this fascinating company. However, she did not wish to annoy her stern, handsome guardian on her first night under his roof, so she rose obediently and smiled her goodnights all round before turning to Serafina.

'You will come, won't you?' she pleaded, and Serafina nodded, smiling. Then Eloise walked away at Anton's side.

'I am glad the Princess Serafina has taken to you,' he said kindly. 'She is a charming girl and will help you in many feminine matters of which I, alas, am ignorant.'

'A *Princess*?' gasped Eloise, abashed. 'I fear I must have seemed too forward with her!'

Anton actually laughed—a pleasant sound. 'Not at all—her husband, Ludovic, is the youngest of seven brothers, so she is quite a minor Princess. We have several in Vienna, but Serafina is the best both in looks and character.' They had reached the ballroom doors by the staircase where a fat, elderly woman waited, hastily dressed and trying to look less sleepy than she felt.

'This is Frau Schnelling, who will take good care of you. Oh,' he added to the housekeeper, 'see that Fräulein Reisdorf is not disturbed in the morning—she has travelled a long way today. Goodnight, Eloise.'

He turned back to join his guests and Eloise felt a little hurt by his prompt dismissal. Yet had she any right to expect more? At least he hadn't turned her away from his house.

'I feel that I must be intruding here,' she ventured as Frau Schnelling bustled beside her along the wide corridor to a further flight of stairs.

'Don't you worry your head tonight,' said Frau Schnelling, meaning to be kind. 'Naturally the Count—all of us—were surprised to hear of your arrival here, it is such a completely bachelor household, you understand? But he can be very kind. Now here is your room; I think you will find all you require, Fräulein, and I hope you will sleep well.'

She went, and Eloise stood looking round the high, cheerless room where a small fire had just been lighted and gave no warmth. Slowly tears filled her eyes and ran unchecked down her face. She was not wanted here at all—and she would never fit into the brilliant world she had glimpsed below. In a passion of homesickness she flung herself, fully dressed, across the bed and sobbed as if her heart would break.

Tomorrow, she vowed, tomorrow she would beg to be sent back to Carinthia ... or go even if she had to walk.

She had half wept herself to sleep when a thought struck her and she sat up slowly, looking round the bleak, unlived-in room. It was as sad as the hall had been—sad as her first impression of Count Anton's face. No, she must *not* run away. The handsome man and magnificent, lonely house were a challenge—something was wrong that perhaps her father had known about and that she might cure.

To leave before she even had a chance to find out was the cowardly reaction of a child and she felt ashamed. She would stay no matter what it cost. It was fortunate that she had no sense of foreboding, no inkling of just how high that price would be.

CHAPTER
TWO

ELOISE was wakened quite early by the unaccustomed noise of horse-drawn vehicles clattering across the cobbles outside her windows. At home there was only the sound of birds or the soft singing of the milkmaid, her frothing pails hanging from the wooden yoke across her shoulders, coming to ladle fresh milk into the earthenware pitchers placed ready by the back door.

Her youthful resilience was completely restored after the hours of deep, dreamless sleep, and although Eloise lay still for a moment remembering where she was, the next she had sprung out of bed and run to the nearest window, drawing back the brocade curtains a fraction to look out eagerly at Vienna by daylight.

How unexpectedly grey the buildings were—yet how beautiful. Above the rooftops of houses on the other side of Josefstrasse she could see the greeny-bronze dome of a church, while another, further away, had the tallest spire she had ever seen. And the teeming life in the street itself! Carts laden with fruit and vegetables, wood, sides of meat, while one blazed with flowers; a tall white hand-cart being pulled by a man who stopped at nearly every door to deliver baskets of fresh-baked bread and crisp rolls. A gleaming private carriage, drawn by high-stepping bays went briskly by, and the pavements were alive with people on foot.

Soberly dressed men of business in tall hats and gaiters, young milliners and dressmakers in pretty flowered bonnets bearing elegant band-boxes, and here and there a nursemaid trying to control her charges—the boys in tight-fitting nankeen suits with matching four-cornered hats decorated with gilt tassels, the girls in miniature crinolines fluffed out at the hem with lace petticoats and frilled pantalettes.

It must be late! Eloise looked at the sky to find that the sun was quite high, and she flew into a panic. Suppose her new friend, Princess Serafina, had already called and been told that she was sleeping? Quickly she caught up her bed-robe, the only thing apart from her nightdress, hair-brush and face cloth that she had bothered to unpack in her weariness the night before. It was of delightful pale primrose sprigged with flowers and covered her slender body from neck to ankles, held closely round her waist by a wide sash.

She went to the door and opening it, tiptoed on to the landing. There wasn't a sound anywhere, though daylight flooded the stairs and passage, so someone must be up and about. But the air was stale, slightly acrid from the thousands of candles that had been burning last night, so not a great deal of clearing up could have been done.

What should she do? She was longing for a bowl of coffee and some hot water in which to wash so that she could dress and go downstairs. It was a pity that she would have to greet Serafina in the lilac silk, but it would be better than wearing the awful black alpaca again. Now she bitterly regretted listening to Aunt Maria while she was packing, or she would have brought some of the pretty, embroidered peasant dresses she wore at home. They weren't fashionable, of course, but at least they were fresh and *different* ... just until she could buy some new gowns, when she had asked her guardian how much money she had for shopping of her own. But her Aunt had snorted at the very idea.

'You would be a laughing stock of Vienna in one of those! Besides, heathen your father may have been—God rest his soul—but you *are* in mourning!' So the dresses had been left in Carinthia.

She was still standing, wondering what to do, at the top of the stairs when the sound of a door closing somewhere further along the passage made her whirl round in dismay, feeling like a little girl caught stealing jam.

It was Count Anton, and he seemed as astonished at such an early encounter as she was.

If he had looked handsome the night before he was devastating by daylight, the slightly haggard lines etched through lack of sleep merely pointing up the fine-drawn cheekbones and strong jawline. He was dressed for riding in a full-sleeved white silk shirt with a silk cravat under the high collar, a doeskin waistcoat with jewelled buttons which matched his tall riding boots and, slung round his shoulders, a scarlet short cloak. His dark eyes burnt like live coals in his face, and Eloise shrank back as she realised that he was *angry*—but why?

'Eloise!' He strode up to her and, putting his hands on her shoulders as she turned to run back to the bedroom, forced her to face him. 'What in heaven's name are you doing lurking about in a public passage, wearing only night clothes at this hour?'

Her temper flared and she raised indignant eyes to him.

'I am *not* lurking—and, judging by the sun, it must be mid-morning. I merely need some coffee and some hot water to make my toilette in case Princess Serafina calls on me!'

'Mid-morning?' He stared down at her with incredulity. 'It is scarce half-past eight! The Princess and her like rarely wake before noon! You will have to curb your country ways here, Eloise, or even the servants will laugh at you.'

'I *am* from the country, and I wish I was back there now!' She spoke angrily, but there was a yearning note in her voice. 'And please let go my shoulders—you're hurting me.'

His hands fell to his sides abruptly, but his eyes held hers with a glint of sympathetic amusement in them now.

'I'm sorry. Poor child, you are quite out of your depth, aren't you?'

'Yes.' She dropped her eyes so that all he could see were the black silken fans of lashes quivering on her cheeks—indeed, she was close to tears, everything was so strange and unfriendly. 'I'm sorry, too, if coming out of my room was wrong—but I did not know where to find anybody and—and I *cannot* sleep until noon.'

He tilted her chin up with a long, gentle finger so that she was forced to look at him again. 'Do you ride?' he asked unexpectedly.

Tears were forgotten, replaced by a glow of enthusiasm. 'I used to ride every day when I was a child. Then, after my twelfth birthday, Father decided it was unseemly. He couldn't afford a proper riding habit, you see, so I just wore ordinary dresses—but I'm sure I haven't forgotten because I loved it so much.'

'Then I must arrange a few lessons and practise rides for you here. I ride at this hour every day, but I should have no patience unless you proved expert,' he smiled ruefully. 'However, if I receive favourable reports on your performance we might gallop together sometimes.'

Eloise clasped her hands together in excitement. 'I should like that better than anything! I *know* I can please you, because I often rode ten miles or more at a stretch and—and we might get to know each other better then, as well.'

Instantly his face closed like a visor, all trace of warmth and sympathy gone.

'I doubt it. Now go to your room and I will send Frau Schnelling to you.'

With a swirl of his scarlet cloak he went swiftly down the stairs leaving Eloise bewildered—what had she said that was wrong? And just when she had begun to feel really at ease with him?

Puzzled and sad, she moved slowly back into her room, closing the door behind her. She was more certain than ever that there was some mystery about her guardian—a deep sorrow or a close-guarded secret—but how was she ever to find out, much less help, when he froze into remoteness at the slightest mention of friendship! And yet.... Unconsciously her mouth softened and curved into a little smile as she remembered the warmth in his voice, the amusement in his eyes for those few moments before she had suggested getting to know him better. Oh yes, her father had been right—Count Anton was a very wonderful man deep down inside, and surely there could be no man as handsome as he in the whole world!

Her hands flew to her blushing cheeks as she realised that she was falling into a romantic reverie: that she knew, already, every line of his lean, dark face and every look in his eyes. It was *ridiculous*! He was her guardian, possibly twice her age, and a highly sophisticated, wealthy man of the world. If he recoiled from friendship then he would be quite disgusted if she behaved like some silly schoolgirl in the throes of hero-worship.

She pulled herself together and moved briskly across the room to her valises. She must fill her time with positive, practical things and behave like the adult her father had trained her to be—otherwise she would never stand the faintest chance of helping the Count.

Eloise was unpacking when a knock on the door heralded Frau Schnelling with a tray of coffee and crisp rolls, flanked by a dish of deep yellow butter and another holding black cherry preserve.

'I hope you slept well, Fräulein?' she said with a trace of disapproval. 'I had not expected you to wake for some time yet.'

Eloise smiled. 'Forgive me—we rise early in the country, but I shall soon grow accustomed to city hours. Thank you.'

The elderly face softened perceptibly. 'Yes indeed—I came from the Province of Styria many years ago, and I well remember that we rose at six.' Then her small grey eyes hardened again. 'But you will soon learn to sleep until noon like all young ladies of fashion—indeed, you will have to do so in this household, where since such late hours are kept, the servants do not start their daily duties until nine o'clock. Hot water will be placed outside your door in half an hour—Fritz will simply knock, but it would not be fitting to admit him to your room.' After which she withdrew, leaving the delicious breakfast on a small table near the bed.

Eloise was glad that she had made a good breakfast as it transpired that the midday meal she was used to at home did not take place until three or four o'clock in the afternoon, while dinner—far more extensive and important—was usually served at ten in the evening. But that first morning in the House of Satan she found frustrating and depressing. There was no further sign of Count Anton and Frau Schnelling informed her, with deep disapproval, that no *respectable* young woman could be seen unaccompanied in the streets of Vienna. She must either walk modestly with a chaperon or reach her destination in a carriage. So all hopes of exploring were dashed. Instead, Eloise sat interminably in the library leading off the hall, waiting for Princess Serafina to keep her promise and call. However, as her eyes strayed along the bookshelves she discovered many old friends and, to her delight, a new volume of poems by Goethe, and was sitting immersed in this when Princess Serafina was announced.

Instantly she sprang up and ran to welcome this new but evidently true friend.

'Oh, Serafina—you came!' she exclaimed, forgetting that she was addressing a Princess in her delight.

'Of course I did! I ordered my morning chocolate a whole hour earlier than usual so that we should have plenty of time. I dearly love choosing gowns—but my kind Ludovic is so generous that I scarcely have an excuse to visit the dressmakers on my own account. Now—let me look at you properly.'

'Pray don't,' cried Eloise, laughing. 'This poor lilac silk seemed the very latest thing in our village, but it makes me ashamed now.'

Serafina laughed too, but with kindness. 'True, that style went out many months ago—but the silk is beautiful, so you need feel no shame when we visit Frau Mitzi's establishment. Come, I am impatient to get started—you will not need a cloak for the day is so warm.' Her eyes sparkling, she drew Eloise after her by the hand, and when the old butler threw open the front doors, bowing low, she said: 'Fräulein Reisdorf will take Mittagessen with me, so please tell the Count not to expect her until evening.'

Wide-eyed with excitement, Eloise stepped into the pale blue landau with royal arms etched in gold on the doors. Then, as they started off, she had a dreadful thought.

'Serafina! I have had no chance to ask Count Anton how much money I have to spend—I dare not order much.'

Serafina stared at her for a moment, then smiled warmly and patted her hand. 'How nice—how very nice you are, Eloise. I knew it the minute I saw you. But now you must learn the ways of Viennese society. As you are my friend and the ward of Count Anton, Frau Mitzi will be so honoured to have your custom that money will never be mentioned. Indeed your credit will extend indefinitely, it will be such a feather in her cap to dress the latest beauty to join our circle.'

Eloise opened her mouth to protest—her father

had strictly forbidden her to run up even the smallest bill—but the sunshine was glorious, the streets fascinating and Serafina so reassuring that she let her youthful exuberance have full rein. Besides, in her inmost heart, she longed to appear pleasing to the Count next time she saw him. Why, she refused to analyse.

'When we have ordered your gowns we will go on to my milliner—for you must have exquisite hats—they are so pretty at present.' Serafina touched the curling osprey feather that lay on her shoulder, falling from a chic little velvet creation perched high on her glossy curls and tipping down in front on to her wide brow. 'Then we shall go home—my French maid, Françoise, is a genius with coiffure—and until your own gowns are ready, she must alter some of mine to fit you. You are such a tiny creature!'

Eloise tried to thank Serafina for such great generosity, but sheer emotion and happiness made the words catch in her throat.

Gerhard von Eckerman was also riding that morning, unable to get Eloise out of his mind; it was years since he had been thrown into such a fever of desire, but have her he must by fair means or foul. The fact that von Arnheim was her guardian merely added spice to the adventure—what a triumph it would be to carry off his ward from under the very nose of the man he hated so much!

Thinking of Count Anton led von Eckerman's thoughts to Carla von Schernberg. They were old friends who understood each other and now, surely, their designs would be mutual—to remove Eloise from Anton's life as quickly as possible. The strict convention of the times made it impossible for Anton to marry the pretty widow. A nobleman might only marry a virgin, and any girl who was deflowered, even by her fiancé, was doomed to spinsterhood or life as a harlot; but widows could become established, respected mistresses, and that was Carla's ambition. Once installed in the von Arnheim mansion she would be the undisputed leader in the society round which her whole life centred, and she had so nearly achieved her aim before the arrival of Eloise.

Yes, he would call on her immediately.

At that point the pale blue landau passed him—the two girls so deep in conversation that they did not see him—but he glimpsed Eloise and it was enough. No price would be too high if he could possess her and, above all, be the man to waken her to womanhood. He flattered himself that he was as great an artist in love-making as at sleight-of-hand with cards, and he would soon have the delicious girl besotted with love for him.

Count von Schernberg had been a wealthy man and his widow lived in a charming house set in a small garden. Gerhard rode in and dismounted near the mounting-block, hitching his reins over a post beside it. When a footman opened the door he said: 'Please inform the Countess that Herr von Eckerman wishes to see her on a matter of urgency. If she is not quite ready to receive a visitor, I shall wait.'

But it appeared that Carla was more than ready—in fact she was eager to see him, and he was taken straight up to her private drawing-room. There, in a pretty morning-gown ruffled with lace, she had been pacing up and down, her blue eyes stormy. As soon as Gerhard was announced she ran to welcome him,

drawing him by the hand to sit by her on a gold velvet
settee.

So distraught was she that she quite forgot the
courtesy of offering him mocha or morning chocolate.
Instead she cried: 'Gerhard—you are the one person
I want to see! I swear I have not closed my eyes all
night for worrying about the wretched Reisdorf
girl!'

'Then—as so often before—we are concerned with
the same problem, Carla, though perhaps from a
slightly different angle. I, too, have not slept, for I
declare that desire for the girl has raged like a fever in
my blood ever since I first saw her. So—you want her
removed from Anton's life and so do I.'

'You are in *love* with her?' Carla's eyes widened in
momentary surprise. Really, men were the most
extraordinary beings! How could a man like Gerhard
lose his head over a dowdy little thing in black, with
hair all over the place and eyes like saucers? But
immediately she saw what a tremendous advantage
his infatuation might be to her own cause, and she
went on: 'Then surely we can help each other! She will
feel quite lost in Vienna—and you know how Anton
spends all day with his horses and trotting ponies, so
he will never think to provide her with companions.
But you, Gerhard, can be the most sympathetic of
escorts if it suits you! And you are both good-looking
and eligible, so what could be better than for you to
woo her?'

He gave a rueful smile. 'That is where you come in,
my dear. You know perfectly well that no love is lost
between Anton and myself—indeed, I believe he sus-
pects me of *cheating*!'

His blue eyes met hers blandly, daring her to agree

with such an idea. She burst out laughing at his sheer audacity—everyone knew he cheated shamelessly at cards, even though it seemed he could not be caught at it, and this dishonest streak in him appealed to the unscrupulous adventuress in her. In these days it was often a battle—if only of wits—to gain what one wanted, and she was prepared to stop at nothing to regain her place in Anton's life. That he did not love her did not matter at all—apart from his innate animal attraction she did not love him either, but her greedy heart craved the position she would have as his official mistress.

'In other words, you dare not call on her openly at the House of Satan,' she teased.

'I dislike the prying of servants,' he said a little stiffly. 'They would report each visit to Anton and, through spite, he might defeat my aims by playing the heavy guardian and forbidding her to see me.'

Suddenly, knowing she had such a valuable ally, Carla was beginning to enjoy herself, and she couldn't resist taunting him a little longer.

'But Gerhard—have you not heard that forbidden fruits are often the most tempting? Especially with young girls?'

He relaxed and began laughing himself. 'I call your bluff, Carla. You know quite well what is needed: that *you* should make friends with Eloise, although you hate her. After all, you can hardly be turned away from the house now, even by Anton himself. In fact I think he will be most grateful to find you so—magnanimous, shall we say? Yes, you must expunge the rather bad impression you made on the girl last night—a sad mistake, my dear—and become the kind, sweet mentor. Then it will be easy to invite her here for small, intimate gatherings so that she may meet people and have acquaintances when she goes to evening parties.'

Carla's mouth drooped a little petulantly. 'Being so pleasant to her will not be easy,' she murmured.

But Gerhard was triumphant, knowing his point was won. 'But think of the prize! Surely it is worth the highest stakes? And you need only call on her once to issue your first invitation—after that, believe me, I shall monopolise the full attention of Eloise at your "gatherings" and you will hardly notice her. By the by, see that you invite no dashing young men, just two or three young married couples will be best.'

'Including Serafina and Ludovic?' Carla was realising how little effort the plan would really need on her part and feeling a great deal more cheerful. 'After all, Serafina took to the girl vastly last night.'

Gerhard thought for a minute, then shook his head. 'No—I think it unwise. That friendship could endanger our cause, because Serafina, though a nice young woman, is over-protective—and certainly not over-fond of me! My attentions to the fair Eloise might prompt her to interfere—in fact a little of your brilliant vitriol in that direction would not come amiss. Yes, I am sure you will easily convince Eloise that her friendship with Serafina might not be popular with Anton, nor help her entry into our circle.'

He smiled as he remembered the frank ingenuity and eagerness to please on Eloise's face last night. 'If we move quickly the girl will still be too bewildered by Vienna to resist you—after all, your charms far outstrip anything Serafina can produce!'

Carla sprang up, now thoroughly elated. 'Oh, Gerhard, I can see it all! and, working together, I *know* we shall succeed! And how remiss I have been to offer you no refreshment—I will order some immediately, then we can discuss things in more detail.'

Anton von Arnheim was in a strange, restless mood that evening. On the spur of the moment, when he returned home after a busy day in the stables—he was running two teams in the Trotting races in the Prater on the following Sunday afternoon—he had despatched a note excusing himself from attending a party at the house of a close friend. Yet he dreaded being alone above all things, so why such a precipitate act?

His mind refused to admit the truth that he wanted to dine with Eloise and try to know her better. Not more intimately, never that, but explore her interests so that he could plan a course of life for her that would never impinge on his own.

That her face had haunted him for much of the day—that he longed to see her again—was sheer lunacy and not to be taken into account. She had, without either his wishes or hers being considered, been foisted on his household, and he never shirked responsibility.

To that conviction he clung fiercely. He was simply doing an unpleasant duty. Impatiently he kicked one of the huge logs on the wide, open fire which he had ordered to be lit in the dining-hall and coloured sparks flew up, spitting angrily. In spite of the blaze there was still a faint air of dankness in the room since it was rarely used. When he entertained his guests ate in the big supper-room upstairs, otherwise he was out in the evening; and during the day he usually ate a brief

Mittagessen with the manager of his stables at a small Biergarten close by. However, in her thick alpaca dress Eloise was not likely to feel chilled—besides, country girls were always hardy.

That Eloise might have spent the day transforming herself with the help of Serafina never crossed his mind. So when she opened the door quietly on the stroke of ten—having asked Frau Schnelling to tell her the moment dinner was ready—he looked up sharply, then stared in disbelief, scarcely recognising her.

Eloise stood still, her knees quaking with fright. Would he approve? The cold room made her shiver a little, but she clenched her teeth resolutely, waiting for his verdict. Slowly, as if drawn to her against his will, Anton went over and offered his arm in courtly fashion, leading her to the fire.

'Well!' he said at last, no longer looking directly down at her so that she missed the brilliant spasm of pain in his eyes. 'The duckling has become a Swan of Swans, it seems.'

'Do you like the gown ... and ... and my hair?' she asked anxiously.

Moving a few steps away, she pirouetted round so that he should see the full glory of Serafina's rich cream gown, the bodice cut low and embroidered with pearls, while a soft fichu hid the cleft between her young breasts. From her tiny waist the small hoops swung out gracefully, revealing widening panels of pearl embroidery reaching down to her cream satin slippers. Françoise, the maid, had brushed back the soft dark hair, gathering it into a bunch of gleaming curls and allowing one or two ringlets to fall casually on the nape of her neck.

The only light in the room came from the fire and the tall candles set along the dining table and her skin shimmered softly, while her wide, anxious eyes looked almost black. Anton clasped his hands behind him—otherwise he must surely have swept her hungrily into his arms with a passion he had not known for many years. Instead he said: 'You look splendid, Eloise—yes, indeed, the Princess has guided you well.'

The aloof tone hurt her. She had built so much into this moment when she had hoped to earn his unstinted praise and admiration. Now his reaction made her feel very young and rather foolish.

'I—I did not understand we were to dine alone,' she said flatly. 'I thought you might be giving a party, and I did not want to shame you a second time. I will go and change into something more simple.'

'Oh no you won't, Eloise.' He smiled kindly, as he might have done to a disappointed child. 'It will be a pleasure to see you at the foot of my table. Now that I know what a little beauty you are, we must make plans for your life in Vienna; I must find suitable young friends for you—discover your interests so that you will not be bored.'

With every sentence he seemed to be pushing her further away—implying that she would play no part in his own life nor share his friends—and her anger rose. Flushing a little, she held her head still more proudly and looked straight up at him.

'If you remember, I am used to being my father's close companion, and perhaps my interests will not be shared by "suitable" young people? For instance, do they read Greek and Latin? Can they discuss the history of Europe—or know how to study the stars?

Then there is music—I play the harpsichord and am much taken with the pieces by Herr Mozart. Indeed I have a great desire to hear some of his symphonies, which I believe are sometimes played here. *Will* these young friends enjoy my tastes, do you think?'

She looked so very young and defiant that Anton laughed, his passion gone for the time being. 'No, Eloise—and you put me to shame. I can see that you need people much older and more studious around you—and I myself shall escort you to concerts for I like music, too. You must forgive any mistakes I make about you, but being a guardian is a great responsibility, you know, and certainly strange to me!'

Eloise relaxed and smiled. 'I shall be very proud to be escorted by you, Count Anton—indeed, I am only afraid that you will be angry with me for my extravagance today! I do not know how much money I have, and—and I have ordered a great many gowns ... and hats,' she ended timidly, remembering for the first time the enormous quantity of shopping she had done under Serafina's urging. 'I *did* mean to ask you first, but—you had gone riding when the Princess called.'

'My dear, you must never even consider money again! It will be my delight to see you looking your best at all times. Oh, and I have arranged your riding lessons—they will start as soon as you have a riding habit, and to choose *that* you will come with me!'

Before Eloise could express her gratitude and pleasure, two footmen opened the doors and announced that dinner was ready to be served.

Although one of them moved to pull back her chair for Eloise, Anton forestalled him and performed that office himself. Seeing his strong brown hands resting

on each arm of the chair as she sat down, Eloise forgot
her earlier lesson to avoid any intimacy and caught
one of them between her own, turning her head to
look up at him with an enchanting smile.

. 'Oh, you are so *good* to me—I can find no words to
thank you properly, but—I *will* try not to be an inconvenience.'

He moved his hand away sharply and did not speak
until he had reached the head of the long table and sat
down himself. The table, designed to seat two dozen
guests, put such a distance between them that she
could no longer see his expression clearly, and the
flickering candles made it even more difficult to dis-
cern.

'You will not inconvenience me, Eloise, as long as
you respect my way of life.' His voice was remote as
his face. 'I have lived alone for the past ten years from
deliberate choice—enjoying company in the evenings, yes, but only when I seek it. That must be hard
for you to understand, used as you are to life with your
father, but believe me, it is useless for you to try and
establish that way of life with me. I shall, as I
promised, find companions for you as soon as possible. Now—let us talk of music.'

Numbly, Eloise accepted the small vol-au-vents
stuffed with caviare that had been placed in front of
her. Yet, underneath her pain at being so firmly
placed at arm's length, her determination to solve the
mystery that held her guardian an emotional prisoner
was steadily growing.

Anton slept little that night, pacing his room thoughtfully hour after hour. Sometimes he was haunted by a
picture from the past, its outlines dimming a little

through the passage of time, but the pain still vivid as a naked sword in his breast. Then came the vision of Eloise, pirouetting for his approval in the leaping firelight—so warm and young, so passionately alive. *She must not stay here.*

CHAPTER
THREE

WHEN his personal servant called him next morning with a silver tray of coffee and some hot water for shaving, Anton woke irritably from a brief and restless doze, his thoughts still running along the same lines. Eloise must not stay and yet, alone in the world and with small resources, where should she go? His sister in Graz would not welcome an addition to her large family of seven, nor would his younger brother, newly married, want any intrusion.

He dismissed the servant, poured some coffee and took it over to the window, where he stood brooding darkly on the problem. It was for *her* sake, not his own, that he felt she should leave. Firmly he dismissed the longing he had known to take her in his arms. That was just a natural reaction to a very beautiful girl and meant nothing, *could* mean nothing. His heart was closed for ever against any tender emotion ... he enjoyed playing at love with women like Carla, who knew the rules, or pretty girls of the town who asked no more than payment.

But those glorious, violet eyes of Eloise—so young, so vulnerable—had filled more than once last night with unconscious invitation. She had never been touched—never been awakened—to hurt her in any way would be unforgivable. Of course she knew nothing of love, but he knew the world well enough to foresee dangers in their close relationship in this house: a young girl, used only to yokels, suddenly finding herself in the care of a rich guardian who was barely past thirty—the excitement of city life and the inborn flattery of Anton's chivalrous manners if he escorted her to concerts and the like—all these might easily provoke hero-worship which in her innocent heart, could be just as painful if rebuffed as a more mature love.

Anton put down his coffee which had cooled, unnoticed, while he thought his way through to a decision. Eloise would have to remain here, but he must never repeat his mistake of last night—to be alone with her. No, he would make up parties to accompany them to concerts, invite people to dinner when they were not asked out, and give some splendid balls where Eloise would surely win a suitable husband before very long.

For some reason the picture of her in a man's arms made him so angry that he cut his chin while shaving. Then he dismissed the feeling with a rueful grin. 'I'm becoming tiresomely paternal!' he told his reflection sternly.

Eloise again woke early, but with a purpose this time, she was certain. Last night, after they had discussed music and Anton had insisted on a description of some of the clothes she had ordered, they had turned again to horses and riding. He promised to take her to his stables some time to see his splendid stallion, Leo, and his champion team of trotting ponies. Amongst the mares there was one called Mädchen who was gentle and docile—ideal for learning to ride. In her excitement Eloise had exclaimed:

'May I have a habit of very dark green? The colour

of our pine trees at home has long been my favourite!'

'A good choice—but remember, none of your Frau Mitzis who would be tempted to turn you out in fancy dress! No, a habit must be tailored by an expert, and I shall see to it as soon as possible.'

So, being impulsive herself, Eloise felt sure he had meant this very morning. She did not bother to wait for coffee or hot water, but sponged herself from head to foot in cold water, which left her skin tingling deliciously and her eyes sparkling. Then she dressed in the elegant royal blue morning gown that Serafina had given her, and brushed her hair up carefully as Françoise had shown her—the curls were not bunched quite as immaculately as they had been the evening before, but they would pass muster.

There was nothing more to do after that but wait patiently for Anton to knock on the door or call her name. She carefully placed the jacket and hat that matched her dress on the bed and sat down in a chair.

Probably she had risen much too early, but it did not matter. Her mind was filled by such radiant thoughts—the way Anton's saturnine face had grown so animated as they talked, his great generosity towards her, the certainty that soon they would share many things and have at least a measure of intimacy between them. Surely, oh *surely* he must come to trust her before very long and feel able to confide in her? Then she would be able to banish the taint from this fine house, to lift that strange sadness from his face.

On that sunny morning, her young heart singing with happiness, expectation, and a thrilling tenderness for her handsome guardian—she dared not call it more—not *just* yet—the whole thing seemed so easy, so childishly simple in her innocence.

She heard his door open and shut and sprang up, slipping on her jacket so as not to delay him for a single moment ...

His footsteps passed her door and echoed away into silence down the stairs. He was gone for the whole day.

It was like a physical blow, and tears of disappointment, soon replaced by rage, stung her eyes. How *dared* l. leave without a single word—leave her alone with nothing to fill the long, long hours until dinner that night? Or had he forgotten her very existence?

Common sense tried to tell her that she was being wholly unreasonable. After all, Anton had not asked her to share his house, much less his life. But ...

'No wonder he is called Satan,' she muttered. The gold and blue morning turned to grey as she tried to face her immediate prospects. He had not even thought to place a carriage at her disposal, so she was doomed to incarceration in the library while all Vienna teemed with life outside the walls. Oh, it was *unbearable* ...

And so it happened that when Carla von Schernberg called at the von Arnheim house shortly after one o'clock, asking for Fräulein Reisdorf, she was received with something approaching ecstasy. Any memory of dislike quite vanished from Eloise's mind as she ran forward eagerly to meet her rescuer.

'Oh, Countess, how wonderful of you to remember me! How kind! Much as I love reading, I swear this library will drive me mad if I may never go out.' Then she remembered that she was addressing a virtual stranger and curbed the rush of words—probably the Countess was simply passing by.

But Carla was delighted. She had, indeed, merely intended to call and invite Eloise to morning chocolate tomorrow, but since Gerhard was waiting at her house to hear the answer, what could further their plans better than to bear this most willing rebellious victim off straight away?

'Of *course* you shall come out,' Carla smiled. 'I guessed that Anton might have left you abandoned—so besotted he is with his wretched horses, he spares no thought for us poor humans!' Then, deftly, she planted her first barb. 'He is quite heartless, my dear—and I should know! Why, he will declare ardent love, *undying* love one minute, and rush off to his stables the next. One is forced to accept that women play no part in his life—alas, we are just diversions!'

She had assumed a suitably heartbroken expression and now risked touching her round blue eyes bravely with a lace handkerchief. Goodness, how gullible the girl was—she had actually swallowed the small performance whole, and her large eyes were brimming with *sympathy*!

It made Carla feel so magnanimous that she could even admit that Eloise was very beautiful—swiftly followed by the delightful certainty that Gerhard von Eckerman would soon tire of such stupidity. He was a most useful friend and companion, not one to be willingly lost in the toils of a marriage. But this girl was so ignorant that surely it need never come to that! She would have no notion that once a respectable girl had been deflowered her future marriage prospects were ended, so Gerhard could bear her off to that lodge of his in the country, and quench his absurd desire in a single weekend.

Carla positively beamed.

'You shall have a most delightful day,' she declared. 'My dear Fräulein—no, no, that is nonsense between friends. May I not call you Eloise?'

'Oh, yes.' Eloise could not imagine why she had ever had cause to dislike such a charming woman. 'I prefer it, I assure you.'

'Splendid! Because it so happens that a great admirer of yours will be taking Mittagessen with me, and he will, I know, be delighted to escort you to any *divertissement* you choose during the afternoon. Between us we will put Anton to shame for his neglect of you, I promise.'

'But—how can I have an admirer when I have not yet been out from here?' asked Eloise, puzzled.

'My dear, you are a most beautiful girl, and many eligible young men fell under your spell the night you arrived. This one, though, I think you may remember when you meet him again.'

After her morning of frustrating loneliness and spasmodic anger against Anton, Eloise was easily beguiled and enchanted back into her normally happy frame of mind. She laughed at Carla's frivolous chatter, admired her pretty house and was flattered by the frank admiration and assiduous attentions paid to her by Gerhard von Eckerman.

'Of *course* I remember you,' she cried when Carla introduced them. 'You made me feel so welcome when I arrived, and I must have seemed such a frump in that brilliant company.'

'You outshone them all,' Gerhard assured her, adding, 'Except Carla, perhaps, but she is the uncrowned queen of Vienna. Why, even your impossible guardian favours her above all other women!'

But he had gone too far. Eloise was intensely loyal and, though she might have felt let down by Anton that day, he was her generous protector, the finest, most handsome man she had ever met. Suddenly she realised that these two sophisticated people disliked him—that they were deliberately trying to set her against him—that their hints about his relationship with Carla were meant to shock her. She looked straight at Gerhard.

'Count Anton is certainly not "impossible", Herr von Eckerman—perhaps you do not know him very well?' she suggested politely. 'My father considered him a very fine man indeed, and so do I.'

Gerhard was enchanted to find that the violet-eyed kitten had claws—it would make possessing her a little more difficult, but far more amusing. Carla was not so pleased.

'Surely you cannot claim that *you* know him well after so short a time?' She had meant it to sound light and teasing, but there was an edge to her brittle little laugh. She was finding Eloise less attractive than she had thought.

'Of course not,' Eloise replied gravely. 'But we discussed many things during dinner last night, and I believe we shall share many interests in the future.'

This was too much for Carla—in her experience Anton lost no time in making overtures to a woman and then reserved his highly intelligent conversation for his men friends, a fact which had always annoyed her intensely.

'How nice,' she said smoothly. 'Perhaps he showed you all over the house as well?'

'Why should he?' Eloise asked, startled. 'I have a beautiful room of my own and—and may use all the public rooms downstairs. Is it usual to be shown the kitchens?'

The question was absolutely sincere—she had read no ulterior motive into Carla's words. Gerhard suddenly felt a strange urge to protect her, but Carla's spite was not to be deflected.

'Oh my *dear*,' she cooed. 'If you are on such intimate terms with your guardian, surely he has told you about the mysterious East Wing? I declare it has intrigued us all to death! Now that his house has become your home too, I felt sure you would be able to tell us what he is hiding there! How provoking—but you *must* ask him.'

She turned aside to pour glasses of wine as an aperitif for her guests and so did not see the sudden glint in Eloise's eyes—as quickly hidden. Carla had fallen into the trap of believing that, because she was very young and fresh from the country, Eloise was just a stupid interruption to her own designs. But she had made the mistake of others who had not noticed the firm chin on the young face. Eloise was now aware that Carla was her enemy—a danger, too, to Anton. But a secret East Wing in his house!—this roused a vastly different sort of curiosity in her breast to the impertinent, vicious inquisitiveness of the Countess. Perhaps, thought Eloise, this East Wing—if it existed at all—might hold the key to her guardian's sadness, his abrupt withdrawal from any suggestion of intimacy.

Gerhard, however, had seen Eloise's reaction and decided that it was time he took charge of the conversation. Although Eloise enchanted him more with every smallest sign that she had character as well as beauty, he took care to flatter both women equally so that Carla should not become jealous and endanger their mutual plan. Gerhard had never been her lover—nor had any desire to be—but he knew the ambitious Countess very well, and knew that while in her own interests she would help him to conquer the girl, she would not stand for any withdrawal of his attentions to herself.

Using his charm to the full, he encouraged the women to talk of fashion, then sketched in, most amusingly, some of the more curious characters Eloise might expect to meet at balls and parties. Then, during the light, delicious meal served in Carla's smaller dining-room—the main one, leading off the ballroom was only used for parties—he discovered that Eloise was interested in art.

'But how splendid!' he exclaimed, his blue eyes glowing. 'Collecting paintings—especially of the latest Italian School—is my hobby. Dare I invite you both to accompany me to an exhibition this afternoon?' He was careful to look first at Carla, who knew quite well that he collected paintings from no love of art but as an investment, so that she played her part perfectly.

'Not me, Gerhard—I declare your pictures bore me and I shall find more amusement in going to Frau Mitzi for a fitting, and then taking afternoon coffee with dear Heidi to hear the latest gossip from France.'

Smiling inwardly, he felt free to turn his whole attention to Eloise, whose small face, glowing with enthusiasm, fanned his desire to an almost unmanageable pitch. Had they been alone he must surely have seized her in an embrace without care or thought for the consequences. Pulling himself together, he said: 'Then I must do my best to entertain you without our charming hostess, Fräulein.'

'Oh, it will be *wonderful*,' cried Eloise. 'My father and I often longed to see the great exhibitions in Vienna, having studied art as best we could from books and reproductions. Indeed, if we had had the money we should have travelled to Italy. So this will be a rare treat, Herr von Eckerman!'

Gerhard had been pleased to find character in his little beauty, but was not so happy to discover that she had brains and education as well. He must guard his tongue or she might pierce his veneer of culture, which went scarcely skin-deep. His whole mind and soul were obsessed with money—how to acquire it with skill and protect it with acumen. If she bombarded him with questions about artists and styles he could well be lost, so this must not happen.

No, he would take her to the exhibition and then absorb her in conversation about herself—pretend to abandon his own interest in art by offering deep, sympathetic interest in her plight as the ward of Satan. Make her understand that in him she had a confidant, a friend who would never betray her but always be ready to listen and to help—even to rescue her if the need arose. And he would make quite sure that it *did*.

Luckily for his plan, the exhibition was not very interesting. Eloise, who had hoped to see canvases by Michelangelo, Botticelli and Titian, was disappointed to find only works by modern German painters, although she was impressed when Gerhard, frowning knowledgeably, bought one.

'The young man shows promise,' he said easily, 'but I'm afraid you are disappointed, my dear—and I have dismissed my carriage for two hours. So shall we stroll in the Hofburg Gardens, and then take coffee at a fashionable cake shop famous for the most delicious Linze Törte?'

'Oh *yes*—that would be lovely.' Eloise had no idea that it might be considered outrageous for a young girl of good family to stroll with a young man unaccompanied by a chaperon. 'I have longed and *longed* to see something of Vienna, and the day is so beautiful!'

Gerhard smiled down at her. How delightful it would be, and how angry Anton would be with her when she told him! Excellent! He was sure to accuse her of impropriety and she, knowing nothing yet of social convention would feel hurt and outraged—thus driving a wedge between them. How gladly, then, she might turn to her new friend for sympathy and, if she cried, he must be forgiven if he kissed her! That mouth was driving him to distraction already. . . .

As they strolled together Eloise attracted many glances of which she was quite unaware—frank admiration from men, while women tended to raise an eyebrow and hurry to pass on the gossip. But Gerhard subtly engrossed her whole attention, encouraging her to talk of her life in the country, which bored him, then leading her gently on to discuss her reactions to Anton.

'I have known him for some years,' said Gerhard, 'and admire him greatly—a feeling he doesn't reciprocate.' He smiled ruefully. 'I play cards sometimes to excess, perhaps, because my life is a lonely one, and he doesn't approve,' he sighed wistfully. 'If I had a beautiful wife and a real home things would be different, but . . .' He broke off as if the subject was too painful.

'Oh, *poor* Herr von Eckerman,' Eloise responded

warmly. 'Surely no woman has refused you? You are so very kind and—and good-looking.'

'Alas, you have guessed my secret, Fräulein. Yes, the only woman who has so far come up to my ideal preferred another. But meeting you has roused me from despair of ever finding true, great love elsewhere.'

'*Me?*' Eloise was so startled that he realised he was moving too fast.

'Oh, I did not mean it personally. After all, we have only just met,' he said quickly. 'But you have so many of her qualities—great beauty, joy of life and loyalty, so I know now that they are still to be found! You, perhaps, find Anton very attractive? Most women do—but I fear he is like me, and looks for more than one woman can ever give.'

'I am sure that he *is* a lonely man,' Eloise said gravely, believing that, after all, her escort liked the Count and possibly even understood him. 'There is such an air of sadness in his house . . . I wish it were not called The House of Satan, it isn't fair when he is so generous and—and good.'

'*You* are generous indeed to speak of him like that, when he appears to have neglected you so shamefully today.'

Instantly Eloise was up in arms again. Had she disclosed too much about her guardian? 'He did *not* "neglect" me—it was my own selfishness that expected him to abandon any part of his daily routine for me! Let us not speak of him any more.'

'Of course not—and anything you say will always be a sacred trust with me, my dear, I beg you to believe that. Confiding your difficulties—if they come—to women can be dangerous in Vienna, but I just want you to know that in me you have found a true friend.'

She smiled up at him bewitchingly and he thought, with impatience, how dark and lustrous those eyes would become, how willing her lovely lips when he introduced her to passion. Now all she said was, 'Thank you, Herr von Eckerman.'

They had a lighthearted conversation after that, and in the fashionable cake shop over coffee and the promised Törte, Gerhard pointed out many of Society's leading lights. He had chosen the spot well, knowing that Anton would receive many reproaches about the wanton behaviour of his new ward and so have increasing cause to be angry with her. It could not be long before Eloise was forced to turn to him for comfort and understanding, and waiting for such a prize would make it even more desirable.

His carriage was ready, as ordered, outside the art gallery, and when they were approaching Josefstrasse in the growing dusk, he took both her hands earnestly:

'Remember what I said, Eloise—for I cannot address you any longer in formal terms! If you are ever sad, bewildered or distressed I shall be there to help you. Promise you will not forget.'

'I promise. And thank you for a perfect afternoon.'

Gerhard handed her out at the door, resisting a strong impulse to cover her small hands with kisses, then re-entered his carriage as the doors were opened to her.

Blissfully unaware that she had done anything wrong, Eloise was surprised to find Anton striding up and down the hall in a towering rage, still in his riding habit.

'Where have you been?' he thundered. 'And how

dared you drive up blatantly to my door in the carriage of that blackguard, von Eckerman?'

Momentarily Eloise was speechless, all the pleasures of her day with which she had planned to regale him at dinner suddenly quenched. Then: 'But—Herr von Eckerman has been so charming and so thoughtful. I cannot agree that he is a blackguard!'

'I see! You have been in Vienna for two days, and already you feel able to judge who is and who is not desirable company,' he jeered. 'Where is Frau Schnelling?'

She stared at him uncomprehendingly.

'Do you mean that you have been out with that ... that *creature* without a chaperon?' he exclaimed, beyond anger now.

'But it was the Countess von Schernberg who called this morning and took me to her house—she seemed to find it quite correct that Herr von Eckerman should escort me to an art gallery and then to a delightful cake-shop for afternoon coffee. Is that wrong? I have been so happy, and had meant to tell you all about it...'

Her face was so transparently sincere, and now her mouth drooped a little like a slapped child who was being punished for an innocent mistake. Anton felt a dangerous tenderness mounting in his breast, and a growing hatred for himself. He put his hands on her shoulders, all anger gone.

'Forgive me, Eloise. I see now that I am the one at fault. How could you possibly know the rules and conventions in a city so new to you?' He released the slender shoulders, fearing that their slight trembling might tempt him further. 'But please understand that you must not go out again unless Frau Schnelling or

Princess Serafina are with you, and I forbid you to see von Eckerman.'

'Oh no—you can't!' she cried. 'He has become my *friend*—and he is lonely, like me. Why do you call him such terrible names? He told me you disliked his card-playing—but that doesn't make him a black-guard!'

Anton looked at her coolly. One minute she behaved like an intelligent woman, the next like a foolish child.

'Eloise, I had hoped not to have to play the heavy guardian, but you force me to. Gerhard von Ecker-man has probably the worst reputation in Vienna—he lives by his wits, and money falsely obtained from other people. I shall not go into any details, but I insist that you obey me in this. If you think that one real friend can be made in an afternoon then you are sillier than I thought, since true friendship takes a great deal longer—maybe years. Meantime, *you are not to see him!*'

'I have no intention of being rude,' she tossed her head defiantly. 'Whenever I meet Herr von Eckerman I shall speak to him—and why have you not men-tioned the Countess? *She* seemed to like him very much, and saw nothing wrong in his escorting me out alone, as I told you, and she is a very grand lady.'

Anton's smile was tight-lipped and grim. 'That "lady" would do a great deal to annoy me just at present.'

'I don't think she likes you very much,' Eloise agreed honestly, but couldn't resist adding: 'Yet she said you had declared undying love for her!'

She flushed with shame at such an unworthy remark, as Anton treated it as it deserved by turning away from her and ignoring it. When he reached the library door he said over his shoulder:

'Be changed and ready within the hour—I have arranged a small party to accompany us to a concert this evening.' And he went in and shut the door.

She stood quite still, alone in the hall, since the butler had hurried away after admitting her. Her eyes, fixed on the closed door between them, grew dark as velvet and in a tone of awe she whispered, 'I love him!'

The revelation was so sudden yet so complete that she went slowly upstairs lost in thought, for this was no girlish fancy but a bitter-sweet ache that filled her heart, a deep yearning that made her feel ten years older than the defiant, stormy girl who had just behaved so childishly.

She thought briefly of von Eckerman—he had been most charming, yes, but compared to the strength and dignity of Anton had he not been a little too glib? Too quick to flatter her and to make rather cruel, petty jokes about the smart people gathered in the coffee shop? Anton had just shown that he could never sink to pettiness, that he cared deeply for her welfare—and what a burden she must be!—and would not have forbidden her to see von Eckerman without good reason.

But, as she reached her room, she knew despair. Last night Anton had liked her, enjoyed her company and conversation as an equal. But now she had thrown all that away, and from now on he would treat her as a wayward child. And it was entirely her own fault.

Tears were pricking her eyelids when she saw that two dress-boxes from Frau Mitzi lay already on her bed, and some of her courage returned. She must not cry—no, she would make herself absolutely beautiful tonight and behave like the grown woman she now felt herself to be. It might not be too late . . . it *must* not be, for now her own happiness depended as much as his on her gaining his trust and, if God was good, helping him to lay the ghost that haunted him into such sadness.

Although she had gratefully accepted Serafina's blue day gown, Eloise had chosen her own wardrobe in pale mourning colours—white, cream, pale silver and the deep violet of her own eyes. To her delight one of the boxes contained an exquisite silver gown with matching satin slippers and a graceful fan. The fichu and bodice were a fretwork of silver lace, edged with narrow velvet, and there was a matching shawl for her shoulders.

To her surprise a knock on the door revealed Frau Schnelling, looking not only friendly but a little shy.

'Excuse me, Fräulein, but I wonder if I could help you a little with your hair?' She hurried on: 'Before I came here I was personal maid to a young person who made a brilliant marriage and moved to Italy. I am not unskilled, I promise you.'

'Oh, Frau Schnelling, you are an angel!' Eloise exclaimed. 'I fear I have offended the Count today, and I so much want to make a good impression this evening.'

Anton dressed sombrely, to match his mood, but with his usual elegance. In some ways it was a comfort that Eloise had shown herself to be still a child—and a fiery one—so that he could dismiss his tiresome feelings of tenderness as sheer folly. But at the same time there was a strange sense of loss for the beautiful young woman who had been such a lively, intelligent companion the evening before. A woman, against all his instincts, that he might have loved.

It was a relief, he insisted inwardly, that this was no longer a danger.

He had his own box at the concert hall, and tonight he had invited four people to make up the party of six—Serafina and her husband, Fritz von Bulow, a rich youth of nineteen who was to escort Eloise, and his aunt, a delightfully witty old lady whose company Anton always enjoyed. After the concert they would go on to a private supper-party and ball where, again, Anton intended Fritz to be Eloise's official partner. If von Eckerman chanced to be there Anton would see to it personally that he had no chance to talk to Eloise.

While these guests were assembling downstairs Frau Schnelling was deftly putting the final touches to Eloise's hair and, when she was ready, the old woman stood back to look at her.

'Fräulein—you will be the most beautiful girl in Vienna tonight,' she beamed, all signs of her earlier grumpy hostility quite gone. Indeed, Eloise felt that for some reason, she had gained an ally in this great house.

'Then I owe it to you—and oh, how I thank you!' she exclaimed, twirling round for a final look at herself in the long mirror. 'I must learn to manage my own hair but it is very difficult! Thank you again.' She went to the door and it was then that Frau Schnelling dropped a warning that accounted for her changed attitude.

'There is much for you to learn yet, Fräulein—and you with no mother or even an aunt to guide you. But—although it isn't my place to say it—you keep away from that Countess von Schernberg and her like.

She had her cap fair set at the Master, and a lot of trouble she caused here, too. But, praise God, he sent her packing, I hear. If I'd known she had called for you this morning I would have warned you not to go—she won't be doing you any good if she can help it.'

Eloise stared at her, her eyes shining. 'Frau Schnelling—is it true that the Count dismissed her from his life? Oh, you have made me so *happy*—and explained so much!'

Frau Schnelling smiled. 'Not much goes unnoticed here, Fräulein. The staff were full of it after the night you arrived.'

Eloise simply floated to the top of the stairs. So Anton was *not* full of 'undying love' for Carla at all—and this afternoon had all been a vicious plot on her part to discredit Eloise in his eyes! She could hardly wait to explain it to him. But the others were all ready for her in the hall so there would be no chance until later.

As she walked down, a vision of floating silver, burnished dark hair and eyes like stars, they all turned to watch and welcome her. In fact Fritz was so overcome he let his mouth fall open in his over-pink face and forgot to close it.

Only Anton did not even glance at her.

CHAPTER FOUR

BECAUSE Eloise had changed so dramatically herself during the past hour or so, Anton's rebuff hurt her out of all proportion. Was it *possible* that she could feel such aching depths of love for him, yet he felt nothing? Nothing, that was, except anger with the foolish girl she had been that afternoon, which seemed a lifetime ago now.

While Serafina greeted her with a warm kiss and cries of praise on her appearance, Fritz continued to goggle and Ludovic, Serafina's husband, bowed low. Even the elderly aunt bestowed an approving smile when they were introduced. Anton was wholly occupied with swinging on his opera cloak and fastening the gold lion heads that clasped it at the neck.

Eloise kept smiling at the small company, but the glow had faded from her lovely eyes and Serafina sensed that something was wrong.

'You must ride in our carriage, Liebchen, I insist,' she said, after a glance at Anton. She had, of course, already heard about Eloise spending the afternoon unwisely with von Eckerman, but surely Anton was not unreasonable enough to blame Eloise for that? She had had no time to learn the rules of society as yet. Serafina was intensely loyal, and she already regarded the beautiful girl as her protégée as well as her friend, and if Anton had been harsh with her then he did indeed deserve the name of Satan.

At any other time Eloise would have been enchanted by the concert hall: the fine white and gold décor, the brilliance of an audience whose jewels glittered with every movement, the novelty of seeing a platform slowly filling up with musicians which she had only dreamed of before. But when they reached the box Anton placed her between Serafina and Fritz at the front, while he himself sat at the back, as far from her as possible.

Her eyes sparkled again, but with unshed tears, forcibly held back, and she was grateful for the fan which hid her trembling mouth as many elegant opera-glasses were focused on her with eager curiosity and appraisal.

The music, which she had hoped to share with Anton after their discussion the night before, floated round her but, as music can, made her more melancholy than ever. When the interval came Serafina said: 'Come, Eloise—you take Fritz's arm for the Promenade—he is young and new to Vienna too, and will be so proud to escort you.'

Obediently Eloise turned towards Fritz and discovered that although his face *was* pink and chubby, it was a *nice* face and his shy eyes had the hopeful expression of a puppy begging for a bone. With a warm smile of sympathy, knowing only too well how he felt, she rose and took his arm, leaving the box without a backward glance.

Had she glanced over her shoulder her mood might have changed, for Anton, as she moved away, watched her slender silver figure go with burning eyes.

The ball afterwards, a particularly grand and crowded one given at the Kinsky Palace by Prince Ludovic's elder brother and his wife, lifted Eloise's spirits in spite of her heartache. Many palaces in Vienna tended to be austere and gloomy, but the Kinsky was like something from a fairy tale, all light and air. Pale rose carpeting and two slender, curving staircases led up to the reception area, banked with flowers. Smiling young footmen in gold livery added to the air of festivity while, glimpsed beyond the host and hostess, the ballroom was of such a size and brilliance that it quite took her breath away.

As soon as Ludovic had presented her to his brother and his sister-in-law, the first person to hurry forward in welcome was Gerhard von Eckerman, proud of knowing Eloise already.

'I am charmed, Fräulein—and I hope you will grant me the next waltz?'

With a sixth sense bestowed by her new total femininity, Eloise knew that Anton was only a few paces behind, and she answered sweetly: 'I'm afraid I must decline, Herr von Eckerman.' Her tone cooled as she added: 'I fear you misled me gravely this afternoon, and I would not have that happen again.'

Her clear, soft voice carried well, and several women nearby nodded and smiled their approval—word would swiftly go round that Count Anton's ward was charming and had not deliberately flouted convention.

Meantime, with a smile, Eloise turned invitingly to a delighted Fritz, who whirled her eagerly, if a trifle clumsily, on to the dance floor. She was a born dancer and quickly put him at his ease so that he found the rhythm without much difficulty—and after that she was besieged by partners anxious to fill up the engagement card hanging on her wrist from a golden ribbon.

For a time the sheer joy of dancing revived her natural exuberance, but as one hour and then another passed with no sign from Anton, a great longing for a sight of him, for the feeling of his strong arms round her instead of all these pomaded, witty young men, began to obsess her. Surely, *surely* he had overheard her refusal of von Eckerman—in this fantasy setting, he couldn't still be angry with her?

But he was nowhere to be seen. She wished and ached and *willed* him to appear and dance with her. But of course, she thought, if he did not share her feelings then there could be none of the magic telepathy that existed between lovers.

At the end of a lively schottische she and Serafina ended up, breathless, beside each other and the older girl said, 'I declare, I haven't sat down once since we arrived, have you? Let's go and join Ludovic in the supper-room—he and his brother are having champagne there.'

The two young princes were delighted to see them, and both laughed uproariously when Eloise—who had never tasted champagne before and was thirsty—took too large a sip and the bubbles made her sneeze.

The tiny sound made Anton look up from his seat across the room, and at last their eyes met. He had seldom spent such a wretched evening in his life, being all too conscious of the effect Eloise's beauty was having on him, and determined to resist it. Better she should think him still angry over a petty squabble—that way, being so young, she would quickly dismiss him from her thoughts and turn whole-heartedly to younger, more suitable companions who were as fresh to life and free as she was.

Watching her—loving her as, perhaps, he had from the moment they met—he felt old for the first time, old and bitter at the way he had allowed a tragedy of long ago to scar his heart and erode his very spirit, so that he was no longer worthy to give or receive love.

None of this showed from behind the handsome, impassive mask of his face as he surveyed the brilliant scene around him with his usual air of slight cynicism. And, as Eloise stared at him, Carla von Schernberg chose that very moment to join him flirtatiously, her head on one side and both hands stretched out in an invitation to dance. She had drunk a great deal of champagne and had quite forgotten that Anton had dismissed her from his private life. But for once he was pleased to see her and, playing up to her advances, he carried her off to the ballroom with an arm round her waist.

That, he thought with a heavy heart, should make it quite clear to Eloise that she shared no part of his life except as a ward.

It was impossible for Eloise to dance badly, but as each of the princes in turn asked her to dance she felt suddenly drained, weighed down by terrible weariness. Even the sight of Carla gazing up most wantonly into Anton's eyes did not seem to matter any more. Fortunately the ball was almost over, and several people had already left; all she longed for was the blessed darkness and solitude of her own room.

The first turquoise and silver streak of dawn was just showing in the east when Anton handed her, at last, into his carriage. The drive lasted no more than five or six minutes. After a few seconds he said stiffly, 'You did me credit, Eloise—you were quite the prettiest girl there.'

'Thank you,' she said with equal stiffness. 'I had hoped to have a chance of talking to you—of explaining much about this afternoon and apologising, but perhaps the Countess herself explained?'

This last was a mistake, she knew, and could have bitten her tongue out—but she was in the first agonising pangs of jealousy she had ever known. To think of such a shallow spoilt woman, who did not hesitate to say spiteful things behind his back, having the right to lie in Anton's arms, to feel the passion of his kisses and hear the tender, silly endearments only exchanged between lovers, drove her nearly out of her mind.

They ended the short drive in silence, and Anton opened one half of the front doors with his key.

Inside the hall was pitch-black; the candles had guttered out and only a faint nimbus-glow round the tiled stove showed that it still burned, but it shed no light. Eloise stood still while Anton flung down his opera cloak and hat on a chair nearby.

'Where on earth are you, Eloise?' he asked through the darkness.

'By the door. I—I can't see the staircase.'

'Gott in Himmel, I should have told them to leave candlesticks ready—but I am so used to finding my way about this house blindfold, I forgot. Come on.'

He moved towards her confidently. In the dark, where he could no longer see her beauty, he felt certain that he could treat her like a child—a small, helpless creature who had no claims on his emotions.

With a small gasp she was swept up into his arms,

her head cradled against his shoulder as he strode towards the stairs. Instinctively—also like a child—she slipped an arm round his neck for security, but then all thoughts of childhood were forgotten.

She could feel the strong beating of his heart against her breast—feel the rich thickness of his hair under her hand—and her own heart began racing. As he carried her along the passage towards the second staircase he said with a low laugh, 'You weigh scarce as much as a child—obviously you don't share the Carinthian mania for those rich apricot dumplings!'

'How do you know about those?' She was astonished.

'Because when I met your father—years ago now—I lived near Klagenfurt for several months.'

They were nearing her room, but she was so passionately aware of him that she never wanted him to set her down. And Anton, in spite of her light weight, was breathing more deeply; her hair, brushing his cheek, was even silkier than he had imagined, and the sweet freshness of her breath more heady than any scent.

At her door he put her to the ground so suddenly that she swayed, tightening her arm round his neck to keep her balance. It was still too dark for them to see each other, but as her body curved towards him, he gave a harsh groan of despair. The next moment he was holding her fiercely against him, covering her upturned face with kisses until his mouth found hers—hungry, demanding until he sensed her willing tender response. For a few moments his lips lingered with a tenderness that matched her own, then, sharply, he drew away and opened the door behind her, almost pushing her inside.

'That was unforgivable.' His voice was crisp, angry and unrecognisable. 'You must not dare to feel love or gentleness towards me, Eloise, for I shall only destroy you. I think you will have to leave my house. Meantime *you must forget me.* I will see to it that we do not meet for a day or two, when, I hope, I shall have made more suitable arrangements for your future. Believe me, I deserve only your hatred—indeed, I should welcome it.'

She leaned weakly against the open door as his footsteps went away, torn between exultation and despair. Her whole heart and soul had risen to meet the urgent demand of his kisses and she knew that he loved her—that their love had sprung into being as soon as they met and his harsh, defensive words could never obliterate that conviction. But Anton was so strong—so bitterly determined to punish himself for some reason she had not yet fathomed, that she alone must fight for their love until she unravelled the mystery. Only then could they combine to overcome it.

But of one thing she was certain: far from being Satan, he was a penitent in a hair-shirt, trying to protect any woman who was in danger of being hurt.

Still trembling, she made her way to the bed and sat down to think. The faint but increasing light of dawn showed through a small gap in the curtains. Sleep was out of the question.

'A day or two ... a day or two ... more suitable arrangements for your future ...' Anton's words echoed and re-echoed in her mind until she could stand it no more. Getting up she began pacing the room, thinking aloud to shut out the sound of his voice.

'I *can't* go so soon—if I don't solve the mystery that is torturing him then no one ever will. After tonight he will never let anyone get close to him again.'

The thought of her beloved growing steadily more bitter, more lonely and heartbroken with the years brought tears to her eyes and she sank back on the bed, burying her head in her arms.

Young though she was, Eloise had been finally exhausted by the long, eventful day, hours of dancing and the moments of ecstasy in Anton's arms. As her tears ceased her eyelids drooped and her body felt too lethargic to move—even to undress. But, as she drifted into sleep, Carla von Schernberg's words floated through her memory.

' ... the East Wing.'

When Frau Schnelling came to the room with a tray of coffee and rolls just before noon, she was aghast to find Eloise sleeping in the silver dress, now creased beyond recognition. Hurriedly setting down the tray, she went to the bedside.

'Fräulein—Fräulein—are you ill?'

Drowsily, Eloise opened her eyes and shifted a little, her mind still held in uneasy dreams.

'Ill? No—no, I don't think so. Have I slept?'

Frau Schnelling's expression grew stern.

'Don't tell me the Master let you take too much champagne at the Prince's Ball?'

The Master! Anton! Immediately Eloise was wide awake, and she sat up.

'Of course not—I sipped barely half a glass and it made me sneeze. Where is the Count? I *must* see him ...'

The old woman's face relaxed into pity; in her view,

once she had ascertained that the girl was neither a fortune-hunter nor a wanton, it seemed a crying shame that her father had seen fit to place Eloise in this household. She took a letter from the tray and handed it to her.

Eloise stared at the stiff envelope sealed by Anton's heavy signet ring that bore his crest. With frightened eyes she looked up appealingly at Frau Schnelling.

'Why—why has he *written* to me? Surely he has only gone to the stables?'

'Not today, Fräulein. He woke his servant at six o'clock, gave him this letter and ordered his carriage, saying we were not to expect him back until tomorrow night at the earliest.'

Her fingers grown numb and clumsy with dread, Eloise tore open the envelope. Tactfully, Frau Schnelling busied herself with pouring coffee.

The single sheet of paper brought no comfort.

'Dear Eloise,

'I shall be away for at least two days making the arrangements I spoke of last night. A carriage will be ready for you at one o'clock to take you to the house of Princess Serafina, where I hope you may stay for the night. Take a small valise to be prepared. I intend to solve this problem as swiftly as possible and will send word to you there.

'Anton.'

Eloise read the few lines again slowly, needing time to think, then she asked: 'Did the Count leave any instructions with you—or any of the other servants—about me?'

'Why no, Fräulein, not that I've heard.'

'Good. The Count has kindly ordered a carriage to

take me to Princess Serafina's for Mittagessen, but I shall return here by six—I must confess I'm quite tired after last night. Could I have a light dinner up here in my room, fairly early?'

Frau Schnelling beamed. 'An excellent idea.' Her face grew conspiratorial. 'I'm afraid the men make too free with wine in the kitchens when the Master is away—it often happens in a house where there's no mistress to keep order. I have my work cut out, I can tell you—*and* I have to clean and dust his treasures in the East Wing myself; he won't let any of the other servants near it, though by rights cleaning isn't a housekeeper's duty at all.'

Eloise hid her sudden elation with difficulty—surely this was the key she was looking for.

'Couldn't I help you there?' she began, then seemed to hesitate, blushing a little. 'I did all the dusting and polishing in my father's house—he wouldn't let anyone else touch his beautiful books and things. It would repay, in a way, Count Anton's great goodness to me ... and yours, too, for you have been so kind. May I?'

She held her breath. Obviously Frau Schnelling was tempted—but shocked.

'The Master would be very angry,' she said. 'Not a soul will he allow in there, not even his close friends, though I can't see why. Anyway, you're here to enter society—become a great lady....'

'Yes, but I'm not one yet.' Eloise smiled bewitchingly—a smile impossible to resist—and she could see the older woman relenting. 'I am so often lonely here, with my guardian out riding all day. I can't keep on reading in the library, and it would give me such pleasure to help you keep his things nice. It'll be even more delightful if we keep it a complete secret so that he need never know.'

'Well—we'll see. Now drink your coffee while it's hot—I'll bring water for your toilette in ten minutes. You haven't much time if you are to leave here at one o'clock. And slip off that fine dress as soon as possible—I'll see what can be done with an iron while you are out.'

Eloise sipped the coffee, her eyes shining. She mustn't rush Frau Schnelling or her suspicions would be roused, but—*the East Wing*! She knew the danger she was running—since Anton guarded those rooms so fiercely he would be far more than angry if he ever discovered her ruse. He would throw her out and sack his poor Housekeeper as well.

That she might find no clue to his secret there at all—merely stored books and old furniture—Eloise refused to contemplate. There *must* be something else, because her whole life depended on it.

Princess Serafina was as gracious and friendly as ever, but Eloise was tense, and when Serafina yawned a little after Mittagessen, Eloise suddenly had a brilliant idea.

'Serafina—it is so good of you to entertain me today and I know we both should take a siesta, but I am so restless! I could not close an eye. At home I took much exercise every day—walking, climbing our hills and, when I was younger, riding across the countryside. Count Anton has promised that I may ride here—he has even chosen a gentle mare for my use.' She omitted to say that the mare was for riding lessons, because she honestly felt she wouldn't need them.

'But I wonder—if your husband has such a mare in

his stables—would it be possible for me to ride this afternoon, just for an hour, even? I should have a groom with me, of course!' She laughed ruefully. 'I learnt yesterday the wickedness of venturing out unaccompanied!' Then her face fell. 'Oh, but I forgot—I have no riding-habit yet, so it is out of the question after all.'

But Serafina was delighted. She loved Eloise dearly already, but her body felt languorous, her eyes heavy, longing for sleep before the next evening's festivities began.

'It is easy.' She clapped her hands in delight. 'You shall have my mare, Mara, and my personal groom will escort you.'

'But I cannot ride in this gown.' Eloise was crestfallen to find her goal so very near, yet unattainable for such a foolish reason.

Serafina got up and held out her hand. 'I have a closet filled with splendid habits—they may be a little too large for you, but it will not matter.' As they went upstairs she added: 'Engelbert shall take you to the famous "ride" in the Prater Gardens—it is very fashionable, though most young ladies ride there at noon.'

Within the hour Eloise was exultant. True, the blue velvet riding-habit was a little long and an inch too generous at the waist, but she had lost none of her old skill with a horse and the young groom, blushing, complimented her on her seat.

'You are a born rider, Fräulein,' he said as they turned into the famous 'ride'.

The sunshine, the fresh spring air brought a new sparkle to the beautiful violet eyes, and Eloise felt her skin tingling with delight. Even her anxiety about Anton faded in this wonderful sense of movement and freedom. She urged the mare into a canter.

'My dear Eloise—here I am, riding to try and forget your cruel rebuff last night, only to find you riding too. I hope you are taking exercise instead of having a siesta to still your conscience! We vowed friendship, if you recall, but never was a friend more publicly rejected!'

Gerhard von Eckerman looked his very best in an impeccable black habit, shining riding-boots and a white silk shirt and cravat. His mock-accusing yet admiring smile was infectious in her new mood, and Eloise smiled back as he rode beside her, the groom falling a few paces behind respectfully.

'My guardian was very angry—it seems I risked losing my reputation entirely by walking with you alone. Did you not know that?' she asked demurely, though her mouth was twitching with amusement. 'Are you always so wickedly unconventional?'

'No, I swear it! Your beauty haunts me day and night, and the chance to be alone with you was like a miracle. If you were deeply in love, would *you* let propriety prevent you being with your beloved?'

They had slowed the horses to a trot so as to talk more easily and now, finding his blue eyes looking down at her blazing with passionate sincerity, Eloise blushed. But not because of Gerhard's declaration—no, she knew perfectly well that if Anton had not pushed her away last night she would have surrendered to him gladly, with no thought for any rules of society. Even knowing that had he deflowered her maidenhood he could never have married her, since all brides of noble families had to be virgins; she would have sunk to becoming a *grisette*, a woman of the town, for the bliss of one night in his arms.

'No,' she answered Gerhard honestly. 'But I think I could not love any man whose feelings for me made him selfish. You knew I should not be seen without a chaperon—I didn't until later.'

She softened the reproof by a little laugh. 'But why do we talk of such serious matters on this glorious afternoon? Pray tell me about these lovely gardens and show me where the trotting races are held—I dearly hope Count Anton will let me watch them.'

But von Eckerman was quite intoxicated by his passion. Each time he saw Eloise she seemed more desirable, more enchanting. No woman had ever had such an effect on him before, and if it was the only way to have her, he *would* marry her. He could never be faithful, of course, it wasn't in his nature, but he would manage his future peccadilloes with the same skill he brought to his card playing. Now he ignored her request and said:

'How can I act as a pompous guide to the Prater with you at my side? I have just declared burning love for you, Eloise—can you offer me no hope at all? I know you do not return my feelings yet—how could you? But at least give me permission to pay court to you until I succeed. I have much to offer you, my dear. A pleasant house here in Vienna, a fine hunting lodge on the border of your own province, Carinthia, and I am rich enough to grant your every whim.'

For a moment he felt it a mistake to have mentioned the hunting lodge—he had won it during four days and nights of gambling from a charming, elderly Graf who was very popular both in the country and the city. He hoped Eloise would not question him now, in case she knew the old man. The whole event had made von Eckerman deeply disliked and mistrusted for many months afterwards, but he was thick-skinned enough to weather that storm, like many others.

Eloise wasn't listening. The Ride ran close to a carriage pleasure drive, and out of the corner of her eye she saw Anton's carriage passing them. Hoping for a glimpse of him and wondering why he was still in Vienna, she turned her head and saw him laughing down at his companion—Carla.

He did not look up.

Eloise thought she must faint, the shock was so great. Pain shot through her in agonising waves and the joy and colour faded out of the day. With all her heart she protested that Anton was not false—was the soul of honour—yet how *could* he have gone to that horrible woman after their precious moments of love so few hours ago? And told her that he was going away to settle a new home for her?

With difficulty she pulled herself together, though her small face was pinched and white when she turned back to von Eckerman, who was immediately all concern.

'What is it, Eloise? Are you tired—shall we dismount and rest? A groom is considered as a chaperon, I assure you.'

'No, I am quite all right. For a moment I thought I saw someone, that's all.'

Gerhard, however, had noticed the carriage too and knew he must act quickly if he was to win this game. All women fell in love with Anton at some time or another, only lightly, knowing it would lead nowhere. But Eloise was not one to love lightly or easily, of that he was certain, and her obvious anguish at seeing

Carla beside her guardian gave her away. Already, then, she loved the man—and quite surely he would break her heart. That would be the time for Gerhard to strike. Meantime, he must not press his love too strongly, rather pursue the line of true, loving friendship ready to serve her, comfort her and ultimately give her refuge.

That she loved another man worried him not at all, for possessing her was his sole aim. In fact if she returned his love it might be a grave embarrassment before very long—even a woman of Eloise's beauty could become cloying and demanding, and that wouldn't suit him at all.

He reached over and rested his hand on hers, lightly holding the reins.

'I have been foolish, Eloise, and I can only beg forgiveness. You are so young, have been in Vienna so short a time, and I will not rush you. No, I will arrange for some of my young married friends to join us for drives—I want to show you the Vienna Woods, the beautiful Palace of Schönbrunn, so many things; and of course, the Danube which will be brilliant blue for me.'

'Why only for you?' she asked curiously.

'Ah! You do not know the saying? "The Danube is only blue when one is in love".'

Dear Lord in heaven, it will be blue for me, too, Eloise thought sadly and found that she was studying Gerhard's hand and, inevitably, comparing it with the long, sensitive fingers of Anton. The hand resting on hers was so very different, blunt and a little coarse, and she knew she could never bear to be touched intimately by it; she was surprised, too, by the contrast to his bland, good-looking face.

'It is kind of you to take so much trouble for me,' she said formally. 'But don't forget I am in no position to marry for three years without the consent of my guardian.'

Von Eckerman laughed, believing he had at last made some impression on the girl.

'We will not worry about that now, my dear,' he said confidently. 'And if you do me the honour of accepting me, that will be a problem for me to solve.'

Privately he felt certain that it would never arise—things were obviously not well between Eloise and the Count, so, if he played his cards right and saw her daily while Anton was at his precious stables, a time would surely come where her temper would flare up in revolt at her guardian's famous callous treatment of women. And then what could be easier than to persuade her to elope in the heat of that moment? In his carriage they could reach his hunting lodge within twenty-four hours—and, possibly, marriage might not be necessary to achieve his desire if her mood were desperate enough. She would come to him willingly, in gratitude. . . .

'I wish to return now,' she said. 'I find that I am rather tired after all.'

They cantered back the way they had come, and at the gates of the Prater, Gerhard said:

'I think the Princess would not welcome an uninvited guest this afternoon, so I will leave you in the good hands of your groom and resume my ride. But I shall arrange our delightful expeditions and send a note to you tomorrow.'

'Thank you,' she said. 'You are very kind.'

He watched her trotting away until she was out of sight, then immediately made for Carla von

Schernberg's house himself. If she was still out with Count Anton he would wait, since she was the only woman who could help him in his plans—he was popular amongst young and foolish girls, but once they married their husbands did not favour him. Only Carla could think up the 'suitable' escorts he had promised Eloise on their drives.

Eloise merely meant to change from her riding-habit into her own day gown, leaving a note of thanks for Serafina, then have her carriage summoned and return to the Josefstrasse as quickly as possible. But the footman who opened the door announced: 'Count Anton von Arnheim wishes to see you in the salon, Fräulein Reisdorf.'

Her heart lurched. Then, her slim back straight and shoulders braced, she followed the young man who opened the doors of the salon before he melted away.

Eyes blazing with mutual anger, Anton and Eloise faced each other across the room.

CHAPTER
FIVE

'You disobeyed me!'

'And you lied to me,' Eloise retorted hotly, wishing that her heart would not behave so outrageously at the sight of him. 'You told me you were going away for a few days.' Was it possible that this tall, stern man had forgotten their moment of passion already?

'I am not used to accounting for every hour of my day,' he said, a spark of amusement at her audacity lighting his face. 'But I shall, indeed, be leaving to spend a night or two on my estate. At the moment I have left the Countess von Schernberg writing to her cousin, the Gräfin von Holst, to ask if she will take you into her household, and I must deliver it and add my personal persuasion.' His face darkened again. 'But if you persist in being seen in public with a rogue like von Eckerman, she may well refuse to be responsible for you.'

'You say he is a rogue because you don't like him, yet he is charming to me! He has even asked permission to court me—most decorously—and I have agreed. Just because you are turning me away, *why* must you spoil the only friendship I have?' She flung the accusation at him, her eyes blurring with the angry tears of helplessness so that she did not see the quick spasm of pain that crossed his face, or guess the longing he felt to take her in his arms again. When he answered his voice was gentle.

'Eloise—you have every right to try and punish me for last night, but not by throwing your life away on von Eckerman. Can you not see that he is false to his very bones? You cannot seriously entertain the thought of being courted by him?'

'No,' she said honestly, her voice low. 'But then I do not want to be courted by *any* man now. I only cling to his friendship because I—I shall be so very lonely.' Suddenly she looked up at him, her eyes pleading. 'Oh, Anton, if I do as you want and promise not to see him, will you let me stay in your house?'

He took her hand and led her to a settee. 'Sit down, my dear, and don't be so distressed. I cannot change either myself or my life style now, and neither are suitable for you—nor could they bring you any happiness. No, you are very young, Eloise, and made for love; Vienna is filled with intelligent, rich and charming men who will offer you a wide choice for the future. Then you will have marriage, children and the delightful companionship of a fresh young mind to match your own.'

'But I'd rather be with you on *any* terms,' she cried desperately. 'I love you, and you are often so sad—even the house is sad. I have prayed that I could help, that one day you would tell me what troubles you—drives you . . .' She stopped on the verge of hysteria, appalled by what she had said.

All gentleness had left Anton's face. He stood up, looking pale and withdrawn:

'I never insulted you by thinking you might be foolish, Eloise, but I was wrong. Just like any other innocent, untried country girl with no knowledge of the world, you imagine you can play Joan of Arc—march impertinently into any life that does not please you, with virtuous banners waving and some mystic power to change back everything to your own childish pattern.' He raised a cynical eyebrow. 'At least you have stilled my doubts about placing you in a thoroughly respectable household, run by a woman and with her daughters for company. You still have to learn to be your own age before daring to tamper with mine.'

She sat stricken, staring at this stranger who had become the centre of her world.

'I only wanted to help you,' she whispered.

'I know,' he said more kindly. 'But let this be your first lesson in maturity—"help" can be the most dangerous, damaging thing in the world unless it is asked for! Now I must fetch the letter from the Countess and visit Gräfin von Holst—I shall urge her to take you as soon as possible, and when I discuss the terms of your stay with her husband I'm afraid I must point out that no proposal of marriage by von Eckerman will receive my consent, and without it you can marry no one.'

With a small, formal bow he left.

A few minutes later Serafina hurried into the room, looking slightly distraught. Expecting no visitors that afternoon, she had been fast asleep when her maid came to tell her that the Count von Arnheim was downstairs as well as Fräulein Reisdorf, returned from her ride. Deep in her heart Serafina had begun to hope she might be pregnant—the greatest joy left for her and Ludovic to experience—and she often now succumbed to her body's new demands for sleep in the daytime.

But when she saw Eloise all thoughts of herself vanished, and she hurried anxiously to her new young friend.

'Liebchen—what is it? I was told that Anton was here and now I find you alone, and ill!' She sat down and gathered the girl into her arms. 'What is it?'

'I am not ill,' Eloise assured her in a small, strained voice. 'The Count has just told me I am to be sent away to live with a Gräfin von Holst, and oh, Serafina, I cannot *bear* it, for I long to stay with him.'

'My poor little one—so you have fallen in love with him! But it will pass, I promise. There can't be a woman in Vienna who, having met him, hasn't lost her heart to him at first—he is so very strong and hand-some—but it is no use, Eloise. He either cannot or will not return such tender feelings to anyone. Oh, from time to time he has taken a mistress like Carla, but never for long.'

'Yet he must have loved at some time,' Eloise insisted.

'Well, not since his father died ten years ago and Anton came to live in the city. I believed he travelled widely as a student before that, so possibly he fell in love then, I don't know.'

'I'm sure he must have done,' Eloise said positively, 'for I am certain that he has been grievously hurt at some time. Don't you think that might account for much, Serafina?'

Serafina shrugged. 'Can a young student's heart be broken for ever? I doubt it. But now, Liebchen, let us think of your future. I confess I do not know the von Holst family, and they are not of our circle so I cannot call, therefore you must visit me often instead. I expect you will find it is a big family with sons and daughters your own age, and it will be a delightful change from that lonely house in Josefstrasse—why, in a week I declare you will have forgotten this passion for Anton, there will be so much to occupy your mind!'

She sounded gay and Eloise's heart sank: if even Serafina refused to take her love for Anton seriously then nobody would, and she must keep it locked silently in her heart for ever.

She kissed Serafina's cheek and got up. 'I expect you are right,' she said as calmly as she could, even managing a smile. 'But the ride, followed by Anton's decision, has given me rather a headache. Will you forgive me if I change back into my own gown and return home for a rest? I shall go to bed very early and have a light meal brought to my room.'

'I'm sure that is wise, though I had hoped for your company a little longer.' Serafina, wrapped in her own secret happiness, was actually relieved. Eloise was beautiful and a dear child, but there were depths in her character unusual in a woman, and they baffled the young, easy-going Princess whose own emotional needs had always been so straightforward. 'You will see things quite differently tomorrow, after a good rest,' she added confidently.

Carla was surprised but delighted when Gerhard von Eckerman was announced just as she was finishing her letter about Eloise. She had much good news for him—besides, there would be a fine clash of temperaments when Anton returned shortly, and she much enjoyed such scenes when she wasn't personally involved.

'You will never believe how fortune has favoured us, Gerhard,' she cried gaily as he came in. 'Anton

himself is removing Eloise from his house—yes, she is
to live with my cousins almost immediately. Do you
know the von Holsts?'

'Indeed yes—though not intimately. They give
excellent parties to which I am sometimes pressed to
escort a lady if our own circle have no engagement.'
He smiled and stroked his chin thoughtfully. 'Yes, the
arrangement will suit my plans splendidly. The von
Holst family are not gamblers and so do not know my
reputation, which is quite false as you know,' he added
with bland impudence. Carla smiled.

'Then you will find a willing chaperon for Eloise in
the Gräfin,' she said. 'You can call and suggest decor-
ous carriage drives to show Eloise the sights of
Vienna—after all, your carriage is elegant and they
will believe you to be an honest, wealthy suitor!'

Gerhard groaned. 'Must I be bored to death by "the
sights"? I can only endure that torture as long as I may
come here afterwards to be comforted with strong
wine and share the joke with you! And yet—yes, to
win Eloise for a night or two I am willing to undergo
even that.'

Carla laughed, clapping her small hands in delight.
'My wicked, wicked friend! I never dreamt that one
maidenhead was worth so much trouble.'

'Yours would have been,' he smiled into her eyes,
making her chuckle. 'But I arrived on the scene too
late—so now I must have the girl instead, however
briefly.'

'Good. I am glad you have abandoned the idea of
marriage—it would never have suited you. Besides,
Eloise will make a fortune as a harlot afterwards, since
she will be left with no other choice. I might even like
her then,' she added magnanimously, 'for at least I

shall never have to see her!'

Outside, Anton's carriage drew up on the gravel sweep, and the sight of von Eckerman's horse tethered to the post added to his angry mood. Putting Eloise out of his life for her own protection was tearing his heart in two, although honour forbade him to do less, but the thought of her still seeing von Eckerman roused his deepest fury. He could prevent her from marrying the blackguard, but beyond that he was helpless. How *could* she even tolerate his smooth insincerity, much less like him? In a murderous temper, Anton left his carriage and pulled the ornate silver bell sharply.

Hearing it, Carla asked: 'Will you wait, Gerhard? It is Anton.'

'Why not?' he replied lightly.

Anton strode into the room, his height and dignity somehow reducing its size. He ignored von Eckerman and went straight to Carla, who was sitting at her rosewood bureau:

'If the letter is ready I will take it now—I am most grateful for your help in this matter, Carla.'

Her eyes danced as she looked at him. 'You have not greeted my other guest—or has poor Gerhard become invisible?'

Anton turned then, his cold dark eyes meeting the too-candid blue ones. 'I'm afraid that what I have to say is scarcely a greeting—more a warning. When I arrange affairs with the Graf and Gräfin von Holst, I feel bound to tell them that in my view, you are not a desirable suitor for my ward, Eloise Reisdorf, Herr von Eckerman. Her so-called "friendship" with you I am powerless to prevent, of course, but she can give no promise of marriage without my consent, and that will not be forthcoming.'

Von Eckerman's insolent gaze faltered for a moment. He had not expected such directness. 'On what grounds do you base your objection?' he asked truculently.

Anton smiled. 'That I do not like you.' He turned back to Carla well aware that the simple sentence had conveyed his feeling exactly—that of dusting an unpleasant smut off his sleeve. 'So may I have the letter?'

She, too, felt a little disconcerted. It was so easy to plan ways of trapping Anton in his absence, but his sheer strength of character and self-possession reminded her painfully that it was far from easy—if even possible.

Handing him the letter, she summoned up a most provocative expression. 'Mind you, I expect to receive your gratitude this evening, Anton. I have gone quite out of my way to give a glowing account of you—oh, and of your ward too, of course.'

Taking the letter he raised her hand and kissed it, his face amused. 'Naturally you shall be rewarded suitably, Carla—have you ever known me to fail?' Ignoring Gerhard, he left.

The two conspirators remained silent until they heard his carriage driving away, then: 'I believe that I desire him more, even, than you want the girl—we won't be defeated, Gerhard!'

'If he dares to mention my card-playing to this family of yours I will flay him.' Von Eckerman's fear always took refuge in brave words. 'He has no proof—indeed,' he went on hastily, 'there is no proof to find!'

'Of course there isn't—you are much too clever,' soothed Carla, anxious to placate him for he was most important to her own schemes. 'Besides, Gertruda von Holst is my cousin, so I shall sing your praises, never fear—and she rules that household. Her husband is a dull stick who spends all his time in museums and libraries. But now you must go, Gerhard, for I have many things to do before this evening when Anton returns—as I know he will!'

The von Holsts were not aristocrats but very worthy, wealthy citizens who entertained lavishly within their own wide circle, and the Gräfin had hopes that her two daughters would make excellent marriages and lift them all a little higher in the social scale. So when a footman brought in Carla's letter while she and the girls were taking afternoon coffee and announced that the Count von Arnheim himself was waiting below, hoping he might be received, she grew pink with excitement.

'Of course,' she cried, struggling to her feet, which wasn't easy since she was extremely stout. 'Bring him here at once!' The girls twittered round her, agog with curiosity as she opened the letter, which was quite short, and took in the gist of it.

'*Well*,' her pale, round eyes bulged with delight, 'what an honour—and what chances it may open out for you both!'

Then Anton was standing in the doorway and the Gräfin surged forward to greet him. With great courtliness he bent and kissed her chubby, beringed hand while the girls fluttered and blushed when he smiled at them and, as soon as he was seated, nervously began passing him dishes of rich cream cakes in quick succession before their mother had even finished pouring his coffee. They had never seen anyone so handsome in their lives and, for once, both Tina and Lotta felt tongue-tied. Not so the Gräfin.

'My dear Count, this *is* a pleasure. And your poor little ward is an orphan, my cousin tells me? How sad—but how wise of you to seek a happy home like ours for her! Of course we shall be delighted to take her in, and she will be such friends with my Tina and Lotta. Why, I declare they are chattering from morning to night so she will never be lonely; and every evening we either entertain or go out ourselves, so...'

'Meine Gräfin, your kindness quite overwhelms me,' smiled Anton in an attempt to stop the flow. 'But I had hoped to find your husband at home so that we could discuss money matters before you come to a decision.'

'Oh, Hermann!' She dismissed him with a flick of the hand. 'He is always so buried in his ancient history that he leaves all such matters to me.'

Suddenly she realised that they would stand a greater chance of being invited to the Count's house if he *did* know her husband, so she went on: 'However, he is always here for Mittagessen—perhaps you and your ward would take it with us tomorrow at three o'clock? You and Hermann shall take a glass of wine together in his library while the girls and I get to know dear little—Eloise, is that her name?'

'Yes, it is, and we shall be delighted.'

'Was her late father a nobleman?' she asked. After all, such details were important.

'A magnificent man—a very great scholar, Gräfin.' With amusement at her snobbery, Anton saw her wondering if this meant that Franz Reisdorf had even been a Prince? For she could not ask again. He went on smoothly, changing the subject: 'Eloise will have an excellent personal allowance, and I leave the buying of any gowns or other personal things she may need in your capable hands, Gräfin. Simply have the bills sent to my lawyer, whose address I shall give your husband. Now I must delay you no longer.' He put down his coffee cup and rose. 'It was charming of you to receive me without warning, and I look forward to furthering our acquaintance tomorrow.'

Again he kissed her hand and smiled devastatingly at the girls who each dropped a small curtsey, quite overcome. Then, blessedly, he was outside in the fresh air again, ordering his driver to take him to the stables.

My poor Eloise, he thought wryly, the place is like a nest filled with fledgelings! But a good family home and young company was what he wanted for her, and his decision, once made, never altered. In a week or so she might be twittering too, and it was a much more natural life for her than she had had so far.

And yet...

Disturbingly, being with his horses and ponies failed to absorb him as much as usual. Removing Eloise from his house and his life was essential for her sake—but removing her from his heart was now impossible.

He lingered on after the stable lads had finished work, the soft light from lanterns making the well-groomed coats of the animals glow. His stallion, Leo, tossed his head and whinnied gently in greeting, and Anton went in to his stall to pat his neck.

'Sorry, old boy—I'd meant to ride you out to the estate this evening, but it would mean coming back early tomorrow as things are.'

He wondered what he should do. He was restless,

and had told the servants in Josefstrasse that he would be away. Eloise was staying with Serafina, who would have comforted her by now; his words to her had been harsh and her pale, stricken face haunted him. But it was the only way. She *must not* continue to believe that she loved him. . . .

He took off his elegant black cloak lined with scarlet satin and pulled down a heavy grey woven one that hung on a peg for his use on cold early-morning gallops. He would walk, probably all night, calling in at a Bierhaus now and then for a stein of lager and, if he was weary enough, rest his arms on a table in one of them and sleep for a few hours as poor men did. The grey cloak completely hid his smart clothes and, to make doubly sure that he did not attract footpads or robbers, he pulled a matching ancient hat over his shining black hair and tugged it well down over his brows.

Outside, he dismissed his carriage, adding to his driver:

'I shall not be at home tonight, so when you've bedded down the two horses go into the kitchen and have wine with the others.'

The man smiled and touched his hat respectfully. All his servants admired the Master and were proud of his title 'Count Satan'. Now he was obviously off for another night of devilry in the city, and there would be envious, salacious talk amongst the servants about his imagined orgies.

It was eight o'clock and Anton found his feet taking him towards Serafina's house; it would give him anguish but strange satisfaction to pass as close as possible to Eloise.

At nine o'clock the Gräfin was giving her husband a glowing account of Anton's visit, and also giving him firm instructions about the price to ask for Eloise's board and lodging.

'I know we live extremely well, Hermann, but the girl is used to the very best—we want her to take good reports of her treatment here back to her guardian. A few invitations to his mansion will be a fine introduction to young aristocrats for the girls!'

Hermann von Holst nodded and ceased to listen as she chattered on. He was many years older than his wife and always glad when she was pleased, but he wished she would leave him in peace now—there were several things he wanted to look up in the massive books in his library.

On the other side of Vienna, the Gräfin's cousin, however, was in a raging temper. Assured that Anton would return to her that evening, she had planned a delicious, intimate supper with her finest wines. Then Carla had driven her maid almost frantic as she decided first on one gown then another until the room was strewn with discarded silks and brocades. Her coiffure, too, had to be re-arranged three times before she was satisfied. But at last, serene and scented, she had sailed downstairs to her small salon where Anton must soon join her.

Instead, a footman had knocked at the door and brought in a small, beautifully wrapped and sealed package from a famous jeweller in the Graben. What a charming gesture to send an expensive gift ahead of him! Then, as she opened it, she saw the card and gasped:

'*You will agree, I think, that this is a fitting reward—Anton.*'

So he wasn't coming after all. Her eyes turned to granite as she drew out an exquisite emerald necklace—then, in fury, flung it across the room.

When Frau Schnelling brought Eloise a light, delicious meal in her bedroom she said anxiously: 'I hope the servants won't make too much noise and disturb you, Fräulein, but fortunately your door is thick. I'll come for your tray later and then go early to my own room. I enjoy a glass or two of wine myself now and then—but not in rowdy company!'

When she had eaten Eloise sat by the fire thinking about the queer determination that possessed her more and more strongly as the evening wore on. So strongly, in fact, that suppressed excitement had temporarily overcome her sadness.

After bringing her meal Frau Schnelling came back to fetch her tray and Eloise could hear the other servants' distant laughter from downstairs through the open door.

'You have been so kind—thank you,' she smiled. 'But I find I am not sleepy yet. Would it be possible for me to have a candelabrum so that I may read a little?' At the old woman's expression of astonishment she went on: 'I know it is extravagant, but I have one or two favourite books with me, and they are better than any sleeping potion.'

'Goodness, the Master wouldn't care if you burnt a thousand candles—but surely sleep would be better?'

'I truly need to read,' pleaded Eloise, 'and a single candle isn't quite enough.' With a touch of guilt she thought how far more shocked Frau Schnelling would be if she knew the real purpose behind the request— to explore the mysterious East Wing tonight, by herself, instead of waiting for Frau Schnelling to take her there in all innocence in the morning. For the compulsion driving her seemed to insist that she must not wait—that tomorrow the chance would be gone.

With a sniff the housekeeper departed with the tray and quickly reappeared with a silver candelabrum and a glass container of tapers. She set it down by the bed and said: 'I'll put a few more logs on the fire—but mind you snuff out those candles before you fall asleep!'

'I promise—and again, thank you.'

Left alone, Eloise lit the three candles then, when they had burnt down a little way, she extinguished two for use later and sat down to wait. She dared not make a move until the house was dark and silent, for if she were discovered Anton would be told, and after his harsh warning to her not to interfere the thought of his anger made her heart race with fear.

And yet—*could* he think less of her than he did already? For the hundredth time she wondered what had ever led her to think there was a strange bond between them—even that he loved her as she loved him, with all her being. While she waited she came to a decision of her own about her future. She would not stay in Vienna, no matter how kind the von Holsts might be, for she would never take a husband now. No, she would return to her own village by the Wörther See and, using only the small amount of money left by her father, find a room some- where—possibly the pleasant one overlooking the lake that Frau Benesch, the baker's wife, let out to holidaymakers each summer. There she would study and teach, surrounded by old friends. And her great love for Anton would sustain her since, young as she was, she knew she could never give her heart again.

Only she must, if humanly possible, solve the mystery surrounding him—the mystery that cut him off from all close relationships. Defiantly she felt that her love entitled her to find out, even though she could no longer hope to help him . . . but now the knowledge would help *her*, and prevent all bitterness.

The house seemed to fall silent quite suddenly. Eloise went to her door, opened it a fraction and listened. Far in the distance she heard men's voices tailing off as a door slammed and they made for their sleeping quarters at the back of the building.

She waited a little longer, scarce daring to breathe, then crept back to the bed and gathered up the two tall candles, lighting one carefully and tucking the spare one into the sash of her bed-robe, tightening it still more to hold the candle close. Then she slipped out of the door, closing it softly behind her.

She hesitated—which way should she go? Then remembering the outside of the house she knew that it must be to the right—and if she was caught she would say she was feeling ill and seeking Frau Schnelling's room. Yes, that would do very well.

Her bare feet moved soundlessly along the deep carpet as she passed Anton's suite, then two or three more rooms—and suddenly it was there, facing her. A large door, more modern than others in the house, with an ornate brass handle and large keyhole. Of course it would be locked from casual intruders, but the key must be a big one and kept close by, so that either Anton could go in at will or Frau Schnelling when she wanted to dust and clean.

Holding her breath, she tried the brass handle just

in case ... it turned easily but the door didn't open. She glanced round her in the passage. An ormolu D-table stood against the wall bearing a porcelain urn ... it was empty, and the upright brocade chair beside it offered no hiding place. Then, studying the door more closely, Eloise saw that it had a pronounced lintel across the top. However, even straining up on tiptoe, her small hand could not reach it.

Balancing her candle carefully in the urn so that it wouldn't drip, she carried the chair over and climbed on to it. At first her hand found nothing all the way along, and she felt sick with disappointment. Then, sliding it along more slowly, she felt a shallow niche carved in the back and, unbelievably, her fingers closed round a heavy key.

Fear washed over her, making her feel faint. What would she find behind the door? And from now on there could be no pretence of looking for Frau Schnelling....

The faintness passed as she got down, placed the key in the keyhole and fetched her candle. 'Anton, Anton, forgive me ... forgive me because I *must* go in,' she whispered over and over again as, slowly, the door swung open before her.

Inside was a small vestibule, thickly carpeted in gold pile. Three doors led off it—a large one facing her and two on each side, all painted white and decorated with hand-painted scenes of nymphs and shepherds dancing amongst flowers in leafy glades. The effect was delightful and very feminine. Her heart beat up in her throat and her hand hovered nervously over the handle of the main door—could there *possibly* be a woman inside? Deranged, perhaps, since she was kept locked in? Whatever lay ahead, it was too

late to turn back now that she was on the very
threshold of discovery.

Holding her candle high, Eloise opened the door
quickly and then stood transfixed. Even by the light of
a single candle it was the most beautiful, luxurious
room she had ever seen—and the quality of the
silence told her that it was empty.

The whole effect was of sunlight and joy—slender
pilasters, delicately fluted, reached from floor to ceiling at intervals round the walls, separating panels of
palest yellow brocade. A large bed, draped with the
same material, had gilded cupids playing on the four
posts, while the side curtains were gathered up into
the hands of a smiling Venus. There were beautiful
ornaments and pieces of furniture here and there—a
gold velvet chaise-longue and two armchairs, a
rosewood bureau and a low round table inlaid with
rare woods and ivory. In a dream, Eloise moved forward to see more, the light moving with her.

Then suddenly she stopped, her breath drawn in
sharply with shock.

The curtains over two tall windows had not been
drawn for the night, and on the wall between them
hung a life-sized painting, delicate, sunlit, with back-
ground of sky and aspen trees.

She was staring at a portrait of herself.

Slowly she went closer, shivering a little now and
almost unable to believe her eyes. The soft black hair
fell to white shoulders emerging from a simple yellow
muslin dress, while a wide straw hat wreathed with
gentians hung on blue velvet ribbons from one hand.
But it was the eyes that riveted her attention: unlike
her own they were velvet brown and a little smaller,
but so vividly alive, so full of laughter that the girl

must surely speak!

As she went on gazing at the lovely girl, Eloise felt her heart grow slowly cold and leaden with despair. This was Anton's secret—no dark or sinister mystery, but his great and sacred love—the girl to whom he had given his heart for ever so that, like herself, he could never love again.

Through some tragedy he must have lost her, otherwise she would surely be here as his wife. No wonder her childish plea to 'help' him had made him angry, Eloise thought sadly. How meddlesome and intrusive her words must have sounded. And no wonder that he had lost control for a few moments and kissed her savagely, passionately; because of her resemblance to the portrait and the fact that she was not this girl restored to him, but only a pale copy!

Oh yes, coming to the East Wing would prevent her ever feeling bitter, since she and Anton were in the same plight—but it had also killed any faint, lingering hopes in her breast.

A small sound behind made her spin round, her blood running cold. In the shadowy doorway stood a tall figure completely hidden by a long cloak and a hat—was it a ghost?

'I. . . .' Her voice came in a small scream of terror.

'Well, Eloise?'

'*Anton!*'

CHAPTER
SIX

She stood trembling as he removed his hat and cloak then:

'How did you know I was here?' she asked nervously.

Anton crossed the room and drew the window curtains.

'I was passing and saw a candle flickering where none should be. Come, we will talk in my study.'

'Oh, Anton, I am so sorry—so very, very sorry. Are you dreadfully angry? I—I didn't know....'

'Come,' he repeated, his voice still devoid of expression. He motioned her to go ahead of him and, once in the passage, he locked the door behind them and pocketed the key.

'Give me the candle,' he said, 'your hand is shaking.'

His chill remoteness frightened her even more than his sudden, silent appearance had done. She had done an unforgivable thing in violating the privacy of this brave and splendid man whom she loved so deeply, and all to satisfy her own stupid curiosity, to ease her own pain. Tears of remorse ran quietly unchecked down her cheeks.

Anton led her into a small book-lined study and indicated that she should sit in one of the two tall leather wing-chairs.

Taking a flint and tinder from the mantelpiece he

set light to the fire then, kneeling, he blew it gently into a blaze with the bellows. All the time Eloise sat on the edge of her chair, her hands clasped tightly on her knees to stop them trembling. At last she could bear his silence no longer.

'Anton, *please*—punish me as I deserve then let me go. Everything you said to me this afternoon is true—I am childish, selfish and, worst of all, I have pried. But believe me, I shall pay the full price in sorrow for the rest of my life, knowing how desperately I have hurt you.'

He sat down in the chair opposite, looking at her pale, woebegone face. He was facing the most difficult moments of his life and they needed all his courage—for here, in his own hands, was the unexpected weapon which would convince Eloise that he could not love her and, in time, might free her to love elsewhere. He ached for her as never before, but his own great love for her demanded this supreme sacrifice of himself.

'I am not angry, Eloise,' he said quietly. 'And you have not violated anything—simply become the one person in the world to share my secret and, by doing so, will realise why I am not free to love you and why my behaviour sometimes seems strange and churlish.'

'Oh, but it *doesn't*,' she cried. 'It explains much, yes, but you are never churlish! No, it will comfort me in the years ahead to know that you are as truly noble as you seem—that, like me, you can give your heart only once,' the tears dried on her face as she went on earnestly: 'But now that we can talk freely at last, I beg you to understand that I no longer wish to remain in Vienna. I can never take a husband now, Anton, it would be unthinkable. So I want to return to Carinthia and live very simply on the money my father left—if you will tell me how much it is? I shall be happy there, studying and teaching—for I have much to offer, I think. And there will be no loneliness, for I have many friends and will make more. . . .'

Agitated, Anton rose and began pacing the room—thankful that she had accepted her own version of what she had seen, but appalled that he was, after all, ruining her future.

'Listen, Eloise—and listen carefully. The truest thing I said to you in Serafina's house is that you are still so young—you *cannot* dismiss, at eighteen, the possibility of a marriage and children, for you were born for love! Oh, my dear, there are so many different streams flowing from the well of love—there is the satisfaction of close companionship, a marriage of minds which often brings most pleasure and satisfaction. I am honoured beyond measure that you believe now that you have given your heart to me—but first love is always painful, and lives in the memory because it is so pure, so unique. Only it should be a foundation for building, not for total rejection of all other experience!'

'I cannot stay,' she repeated obstinately, her chin firm.

Abruptly he knelt beside her, chafing her cramped hands, his dark face filled with tender pleading.

'I flatter myself that I am strong,' he began, 'but now you are laying a burden on me which I cannot carry—although I deserve it for kissing you as I did, because you brought back many memories. So will you make a pact with me?'

She looked into his eyes for a long moment, then: 'I

can deny you nothing, Anton—only don't make it too hard.'

At last he smiled: 'Good! Is one month out of your life too much to ask?'

'For what?' She was bewildered.

'To spend four weeks with the von Holst family—oh, it is vastly different to anything you have known. But it is a wholesome, natural life for a girl of your age—the daughters will probably drive you mad at first with their constant chatter of gowns and gossip, but they entertain a great deal and go to many parties. You will meet all kinds of people—and you have met few so far—and I promise not to hamper you in any way by appearing at the same functions. Will you do it, Eloise?'

He was grasping her hands tightly now to press his entreaty, and he added:'In fact I will spend my time on the estate, so that you need have no fear of finding me anywhere unexpectedly.'

To her surprise Eloise was suddenly completely exhausted. The nervousness and strain of the night had taken their toll at last. But she managed a small smile.

'No,' she said. 'If you go right away I refuse to obey you, for, if I am anxious or unhappy you are the only person I can talk to and consult with. After all,' she reminded him, 'I need your permission for my every move! But if you will stay here, where I know I can find you, then I will do as you ask.'

With a great sigh of relief he relinquished her hands, then saw the shadows of weariness under her lovely eyes and sprang up.

'It is late and you are tired out, Eloise—we will take a glass of wine on the bargain and then you must go to bed! I promise that you will not regret this decision.'

He took a decanter of red wine and two goblets from a corner cupboard, setting the decanter in front of the fire to warm a little. He was so thankful at her acceptance that he did not glance at her again until the wine was ready to pour. When he carried her glass to her he saw that she had leant back in the chair, her eyes closed, too worn out to stand any more emotion.

He stood by her chair, his wine forgotten as he drank in—perhaps for the last time—her beloved beauty: the fragile lines of her slender but indomitable body, long dark eyelashes fanning over the purple stains under her glorious eyes and her soft mouth tender in surrender to sleep. What a little thing she was to have broken through all his defences and captured his heart—but a heart too harshly served and too warped with bitterness, now, to be worthy of her.

Quite without passion this time but with infinite gentleness he lifted her against his breast, carrying her to her room for the second time. She scarcely stirred in his arms, only a small sigh escaped her as her head drooped on his shoulder. She could not wake.

He carried her to her bed, threw back the covers as he laid her down, then drew them over her warmly. With a hand careful not to disturb her he brushed back a strand of soft hair that had fallen forward, then bent and kissed her on the forehead.

'Farewell, my dearest love,' he whispered. 'Find happiness.'

Frau Schnelling was concerned when she came to waken Eloise at midday. She found her sitting up in bed clasping her knees, her face ashen.

'Fräulein—this time you *are* ill!' The old woman fussed round the bed, straightening covers and quickly pouring out a bowl of coffee and handing it to her. 'I knew no good would come of all that reading late into the night—you should have had a long sleep.'

Eloise managed a smile. 'I expect you are right—although I have slept for several hours and I only have a slight headache, nothing more. Anyway, I have no plans for today, so I can rest.'

'But you have indeed, Fräulein! The Master returned here during the night and sent a message to me by his servant scarce an hour ago. You are to be ready and dressed in your best shortly after two o'clock—he is escorting you to Mittagessen with some family called von Holst.'

Eloise closed her eyes for a moment to hide the shock in them. When she woke and thought wretchedly about all that had passed between them during the night she had not realised that Anton would put his plan into practice so quickly. But she should have known him better—besides, in spite of his kindness, he could not want her in this house any longer.

'Now you take your coffee good and hot,' Frau Schnelling was saying in an anxious voice. 'I shall fetch my own physic for your headache—a good country remedy it is, and it works wonders. We must get some colour back in those cheeks.'

Obediently Eloise raised the coffee to her lips but it was too hot: 'Thank you—you are always so kind to me.'

'Tch! Such a slip of a thing you are, you need looking after. It takes time to get used to city life, and you were tired to death when you came in yesterday.'

She bustled away.

In a minute or two Eloise was able to sip the coffee and she stared ahead, wondering helplessly how to get through this nightmare day—the day when Anton would virtually go out of her life for ever. But she had given him her word to try her best for one month—and after that she would be quite alone. So somehow, with all her inner strength, she must get used to it.

The only hope was to be practical—to concentrate wholly on feeling less drained and attending carefully to every detail of her toilette, making each movement fill the moment with importance. Fortunately Frau Mitzi had delivered more gowns, and, with a touch of Anton's cynicism, she decided to wear white. The colour of sacrifice.

'Here you are, Fräulein,' Frau Schnelling hurried back carrying a small glass filled with cloudy liquid. 'Drink this, and then lie back for half an hour until I bring your hot water—you still have plenty of time.'

Eloise held the glass doubtfully—she had no headache, only heartache, and she had never taken a physic in her life. But one look at Frau Schnelling's motherly face and she swallowed it quickly. After all, nothing could make her feel worse, and if it made her really ill it might mean a reprieve, if only for a few more days.

She hadn't the heart to tell the kind soul that she would soon be leaving the house altogether—possibly even this very day.

Anton was waiting for her in the hall, wearing a velvet coat of her favourite pine green—with a pang she remembered that she would have no need of a riding-habit in that colour now, since they would never ride together after all.

He held out his hand to escort her outside.

'You are looking very beautiful, Eloise,' he said gravely. 'The von Holsts will be delighted with you.'

In the sunshine an open landau was waiting, drawn by two high-stepping bays. So they would have no privacy during the drive and she was grateful, for there was no more to say between them.

The von Holst house astonished Eloise—she had never seen anything so fussily feminine in her life. Everything seemed to be strawberry pink, even the servants' liveries, and Bohemian glass vases filled with hothouse flowers stood everywhere, their feet resting on lacy, beribboned mats. As a footman ushered them upstairs through air redolent with the scent of roses and carnations she glanced at Anton enquiringly, but he was looking straight ahead.

In the large salon the Gräfin, upholstered in turquoise silk and pearls, waited to welcome them, and when Anton had kissed her hand and introduced Eloise, he was directed on to the library, where the Graf was waiting to talk business with him and take wine.

Then Eloise found herself almost smothered in a maternal embrace as the Gräfin murmured: 'You poor, poor little girl—we shall do all we can to make you feel like another daughter here—won't we, girls?'

Tina and Lotta hung back shyly for once. The small, slender figure of Eloise, so trim in her white gabardine and elegant hat, over-awed them. Surely, she couldn't possibly be their own age?

But the Gräfin, massive, motherly and quite insensitive to atmosphere, would have none of that. Sipping a glass of sweet apricot cordial, she soon had her daughters chattering away as she described a quite breathtaking programme of evening functions that lay ahead, ending:

'And tonight I have arranged a fête here in your honour, my dear—it will be nice for you to meet some of our friends.'

'It is most kind of you,' said Eloise, still rather overcome. 'But—surely I shall not be here tonight? I have not packed, and . . .'

'*Packed?*' The Gräfin laughed. 'My dear child, a gentlewoman doesn't pack—the Count's servants will do that for you, and your baggage can be sent round in a carriage!'

'Oh yes, you *must* be here this evening,' urged Tina. 'Our Mütti has planned the prettiest fête you can imagine!'

'And all done since yesterday—especially for you!' added Lotta proudly.

'Of course she will be here,' the Gräfin said firmly, then turned to Eloise, beaming. 'And you must call me Mütti, too, for I declare you will be as dear to me as my own two girls. You shall tell me all about yourself later on, for we have no secrets from each other here—life's little joys and sorrows are all shared, I promise you.'

Eloise managed to smile although she was shrinking inwardly with distaste, but the Gräfin took her silence as gratitude. Really, she thought, it was all *most* satisfactory—this pale, scrawny little creature with her big eyes would be no rival to the charms of Tina and Lotta with their blonde curls, pretty curves and pink and white complexions. And the connection with handsome Count von Arnheim was quite delightful socially. Perhaps he might even be persuaded to attend the fête?

Unable to believe, yet, that this place was already her home, Eloise sat letting the cheerful prattle flow over her. How *could* she stand this claustrophobic atmosphere that already began to feel like fighting for breath inside a sea of pink marshmallow? And as to confiding in the Gräfin...

She fought down a sudden longing to scream—to break through the cloying sweetness and shock them all. Then run and run and run, with the wind blowing through her hair. Then she remembered her solemn promise to Anton and, over and over in her mind she repeated: 'But only for a month—only four weeks—just twenty-eight days and Anton can ask no more of me.'

At which point the door opened and he and the Graf came in, their talk about her future settled. Anton was immediately monopolised by the Gräfin and her girls, but the Graf came and shyly sat beside her. He was small and elderly with bright intelligent eyes and a gentle voice.

'I hope you will be happy here, my dear,' he said. 'From what your guardian has been telling me, perhaps we shall enjoy talking together of books sometimes—when you are not too busy, of course.'

With a lump in her throat at this unexpected kindness, Eloise felt a flicker of warmth and hope steal back into her heart.

As soon as the meal was over Anton rose and made courteous excuses to leave. He was sorry, but he could not attend the fête that evening, but hoped to accept another invitation later on. His goodbyes to Eloise were as charming and formal as to the others and she did not raise her eyes, afraid to let him see the panic in them at this final break.

The Graf patted her hand, sensing her distress, and said: 'He does not live very far away, my dear—you will often see him.'

Before she could answer the Gräfin pushed back her chair and began shooing the three girls out of the room and upstairs like so many young chickens.

'Come along now, all of you, it's past four o'clock and you must all have a siesta so as to look your best tonight. Show Eloise to her room—I've ordered her to be put next door to you, so that you can all pop in and out whenever you like; I know how young girls love to laugh and chatter before and after these parties.' She smiled at Eloise. 'We shan't let you feel lonely, my dear!'

With a sinking heart at such a dire prospect, Eloise thanked her politely. Times of quiet solitude were as necessary to her as breathing.

When they were alone the Gräfin turned to her husband.

'Well? Did Count Anton agree to our terms for her stay? I hope you didn't weaken, Hermann.'

He sighed: 'No, my dear—in fact he has been more than generous. He——' The old man had been going on to tell his wife that Gerhard von Eckerman was not to be encouraged to call on them any longer, but, highly satisfied, the Gräfin was already sailing out towards her own siesta.

For the second time that day Eloise pleaded a headache when Tina and Lotta, their shyness quite gone, showed every sign of staying in her room, longing to ask many questions about her handsome guardian and discuss the forthcoming party.

'Let me sleep first,' she begged, 'or I declare I shall not feel well enough to come down at all.'

'Oh, but you *must*,' Lotta urged, drawing her sister towards the door. 'Mütti has gone to much trouble for you....'

Eloise slipped out of her white gabardine and lay down in her petticoats, but she was too much on edge to sleep, her mind returning again and again to the portrait in the East Wing of the girl who had stolen Anton's heart. Had the girl been tall and fair the pain would have just been bearable—but for it to resemble her so strongly that Anton could scarce endure to see her was cruel indeed.

She was thankful when her valises and the dress-boxes from Frau Mitzi arrived soon after five. She smilingly refused the offer of a pretty little maid to unpack for her, saying that she would enjoy hanging the gowns for herself. At last there was something positive to do.

Only she wasn't left in peace for long. The girls had heard the footmen coming along the passage and within minutes they surged into her room, agog to examine all the gowns and hats brought by Eloise.

Resigned, she welcomed them in with good grace, then wished she might have had five minutes more on her own, because on top of her larger valise lay a small package. Taking it to the window and turning so that the girls could not see her face, she held it for a moment—was it a parting gift from Anton? Then quickly she tore off the wrappings: inside was a small bottle and a note written in childish script:

'Gnädige Fräulein,
    'It is sad that you go. The house will seem most

empty. Please accept this physic in case of headaches.

'Your faithful servant. L. Schnelling.'

Eloise was deeply touched, but this was no time for tears. Tina and Lotta were already unpacking her things eagerly with squeals of delighted admiration.

'Please, Eloise—may we try on some of the gowns? Oh, we will not fasten them for they will be too tight, but just to see the effect?' Tina pleaded.

'Of course you can.' What use to refuse? These two were destined to be her companions for the next twenty-eight days—she found that the time sounded shorter counted in days rather than weeks—and, when she left for the country they should have all the grand gowns if they wished, for she would have no place for them in her quiet life.

When they left her, flushed and excited, to dress for the fête, Eloise chose a very simple lilac silk gown to wear herself. She did not worry overmuch about her hair, either, brushing back the silky strands quite simply and tying them with a lilac ribbon. She had no wish to appear beautiful nor to attract the attention of any man.

Tina and Lotta were ready before her and too impatient to wait.

'We are both in love, you see,' giggled Lotta, 'and with two brothers! Oh, they are so handsome and well-connected——'

'Mütti likes them, too,' went on Tina, 'and they have sworn to arrive early so as to fill in our dance cards before the other guests have a chance. Isn't that romantic?'

Eloise delayed until she heard faint strains of music

and the sound of many voices below. At the foot of the stairs she found the Graf waiting for her.

'How charming you look, my child,' he said, tucking her hand into the crook of his arm. 'My wife and daughters are splendid women, you know, splendid—but you must not let them overwhelm you. I wanted this chance to tell you that whenever you wish to read in peace you are welcome to use my library.' His eyes twinkled. 'I spend most of the day in museums, consulting historical archives, but not after six o'clock! At that hour I like to be alone with my Meerschaum pipe, and the smell of tobacco would not be seemly in your pretty hair.'

In spite of a lingering weariness Eloise gave him a dazzling smile of gratitude. At least there was one friend in this house! Her violet eyes glowed back to radiant life and the old Graf felt sudden misgivings. All the time that they had been changing for the evening his wife had been in and out of his dressing-room, bursting with pleasure that Eloise was such a plain little thing.

'No danger to our girls at all when it comes to finding a husband! Gott sei Dank, we have been blessed indeed—and with such generous payment, too!'

But she was wrong—God had handed them a very great beauty, and he foresaw much trouble ahead. Besides, in her elation the Gräfin had given him no chance to broach the subject of von Eckerman.

Now, however, he smiled warmly back at Eloise. 'I am a dull stick and no dancer, but I have a fancy that tonight you may feel overcome in your new surroundings amongst strangers.' He led her to a table just inside the ballroom. 'If you wish to slip away to bed before the end, from here it will be easy.'

Eloise was enchanted by the scene. A fête was not as overcrowded as a ball. Tables for six or eight people were set round the edge of the ballroom, framed in leafy bowers with pretty floral arrangements and floral favours, too, for the women—hers was a porcelain brooch shaped like a posy of edelweiss and gentians. Dancing was not continuous, either, as there were singers and conjurors to entertain in between while courses of the supper were served.

'Oh, it is beautiful!' she exclaimed as the Graf handed her to her chair towards the back of their bower and introduced her to the other occupants—two pleasant young couples who knew nothing about her until the Graf explained that she was a visitor new to Vienna. Then, as the first course of supper was served, they eagerly described many of the sights she should see. In this company Eloise relaxed and found that she was actually hungry.

Suddenly something—some instinct—drew her attention to the door through which two new arrivals were coming, a young woman and her tall, fair escort whose eyes were already roaming the room. Overjoyed at seeing the familiar face, she half rose from her seat.

'Gerhard!' she cried, and after a swift word to his companion, von Eckerman came towards her with a brilliant smile.

'Eloise, I only just heard that you have come to live here—how fortunate that Frau von Schreider asked me to accompany her as her husband is unwell.' Tactfully he turned with a formal bow to the Graf: 'Forgive me for greeting Fräulein Reisdorf before you, mein Graf, but she and I are old friends already.'

The old man did not return his smile. 'I believe we

have had the pleasure of your company here before, Herr...?'

'von Eckerman—Gerhard von Eckerman.'

'Ah, yes, of course. Now somebody was telling me lately that you are a great hand at cards. I regret to tell you that we do not indulge in such games in this house. But I detain you. Your companion is waiting to greet her hostess—you will find my wife at the top table.'

Slightly disconcerted, Gerhard bowed again and moved away to lead Frau von Schreider across to the Gräfin. Surely the Graf could know nothing of his reputation in certain circles? Or had Count Anton brought false accusations already? He decided to waste no time in charming the Gräfin and suggesting some enjoyable carriage drives for herself and Eloise—and, of course, her two daughters if they liked. The Gräfin needed little persuading—she had always regarded Gerhard favourably, knowing that he often moved in exalted social circles. She begged him to sit beside her for a few minutes to discuss plans as the dancing started again.

Eloise and the Graf were left alone at their table and she looked at him curiously. She felt she had known him for a long time, although it was only hours.

'You don't like Herr von Eckerman—why?' she asked bluntly.

'Put it another way—I would not permit him to court one of my daughters.'

'But *why*?' she insisted. 'He is very good-looking and extremely kind...'

'And he's a rogue,' the old man finished for her. 'To be fair, your guardian told me today that he does not favour the man as a suitor for you, either, and I was not surprised. I have never cared for him, although my wife seems to invite him occasionally, and a man who is disliked by other men is usually flawed in some way.'

Eloise was silent, unwilling to answer. Honesty forced her to admit that both Anton and now the Graf, whom she respected so much, could not be wrong ... and she remembered Gerhard's hands, that were so coarse compared to his face that they had slightly repelled her. Yet, obstinately, she refused to give in meekly and abandon him as a friend. What harm could that do, even if he *was* a rogue in some ways? She looked up at the Graf and smiled.

'I promise that you need not worry on my account. I shall never even consider Gerhard as a husband, but I do value him as a friend. I beg you not to forbid that.'

'Hm,' said the Graf, none too pleased. His eyes missed nothing and he had known the moment Gerhard looked at Eloise that even if her feelings were merely friendly at present, his most certainly were not. He resolved to have a serious talk to the Gräfin on the subject, for he did not want to turn Eloise against him on her very first evening. He got up.

'Well, since your "friend" will soon be back to dance with you, I shall betake myself off for a quiet pipe and then bed. Goodnight, my dear—and don't dismiss my words, will you?'

'I have already promised,' she said quietly.

When Gerhard came to claim her for a minuet some ten minutes later she felt an upsurge of warmth towards him. She could not understand why Anton and the Graf were so set against him. In fact Carla's prediction was beginning to come true—that forbidden fruit held great magnetism for young girls.

Gerhard recognised the subtle change in her and his hopes rose. Now that she was safely away from Anton's watchful eye perhaps she would cling to him tenderly quite soon. For this house and the silly von Holst women could not be to her liking at all.

To Eloise Gerhard's adoring glances and charming smile were like cooling balm in her loneliness: her life was in ruins and she dared not look into the bleak future. Her heart was still numbed and shattered at the final loss of Anton, but the searing pain ahead when that numbness wore off would not possess her just yet. Meantime, this friendship was all she had.

'Oh, Gerhard, you cannot know how pleased I am to see you,' she murmured as she drifted, feather-like, on his arm with a willingness that set his pulses racing.

'I shall always be there when you need me,' he promised. 'Indeed I have just made delightful plans with the Gräfin for your pleasure. We shall see much of each other, I think.'

He let his cheek brush briefly against her soft hair as he led her back to her table—his urgent desire could not be curbed much longer.

CHAPTER
SEVEN

THE Graf von Holst waited up for his wife, feeling duty bound to both Anton and Eloise to give her instructions about von Eckerman. But the Gräfin, who had indulged a little too freely in wine as well as food, was impatient for bed.

'You talk absolute nonsense, Hermann,' she snapped. 'What do you know of society and what goes on? You, with your nose stuck in dusty old books all day long! Herr von Eckerman is wealthy, charming and received everywhere, so do go to bed and leave things to me!'

'But Count Anton himself asked me to discourage the man.'

'Tch! He should be glad that anyone shows an interest in the dull girl—hardly any of our other guests asked her to dance tonight, she appeared so pale and standoffish. If the Count disapproves of Herr von Eckerman so much he can give *me* his reasons—why, the young man is quite putting himself out to take me and all the three girls on pleasure drives during the next fortnight!' And she went into her bedroom and slammed the door.

The Graf sighed. It was useless to argue with Gertruda and he rarely tried; long ago he had realised that the marriage was the folly of a middle-aged man losing his senses over a statuesque young blonde with whom he had nothing in common. After that, he set about building a peaceful life for himself outside their home, which pleased her, too, as he was always most generous with his money.

He was not prepared to destroy all that for Eloise—besides, he comforted himself, she herself had promised that she would never marry von Eckerman. On which thought he went to bed himself.

Six days after he had parted from Eloise, Anton was riding Leo through the Vienna Woods. His mood was restless and stormy and he found he could settle to nothing; the social round bored him—as it had done inwardly for a long time—so that he refused all invitations and did no entertaining himself. He spent more and more time with his horses, so that callers at Josefstrasse were always told that he was out.

Strong as he was, and unwavering about his decision to send Eloise away, the nights were torment. He had scorned and mistrusted women for so many years that he had believed himself invulnerable—complete master of himself and his emotions. Then Eloise had walked through his ballroom door in her black alpaca and, unconsciously, walked through all his defences, making matchwood of them under her small, slippered feet.

Too late. In his earlier pain he had hurt too many people, broken too many hearts without caring, and he could not now accept her purity and innocence, the glorious love in her violet eyes. So, through the long nights, he reasoned with himself—justified himself. But the hours dragged by; he longed to be away on his estate, to a house that was not haunted by Eloise at every turn and where he could absorb himself in the busy country life.

In three more weeks he would be free to go—she must surely have settled by then, surrounded by youthful gaiety and adoring young men, and her thoughts of him would fade to a dim, fond memory.

He was riding amongst the trees when he saw von Eckerman's carriage bowling along one of the Pleasure Drives. Anton reined in and looked down from a vantage point where he could not be seen.

Eloise was sitting well forward, looking out at a bluebell glade with von Eckerman's head close to hers as he pointed to it—but his eyes were on her face. She looked better and happier than when Anton had taken leave of her, and he tried to quell his rising anger. The outing was perfectly proper, since the large form of the Gräfin loomed on the seat beside Eloise so no one could think she was unchaperoned.

He sat still, watching the carriage out of sight, until Leo pawed the ground impatiently, wanting to be off on their usual gallop. But Anton's anger grew. The Graf had evidently ignored his instructions or, more likely, the Gräfin had overridden them. For the expression on von Eckerman's face as he gazed at Eloise had been unmistakable, even from this distance: passionate lust. And she had seemed quite content to have him so close.

Furious, Anton turned Leo's head round and cantered back to Vienna, straight to Carla's house. He would see the Graf himself, but she must deal with her cousin.

Carla, however, had not forgiven Anton for the emerald necklace and his avoidance of her. Twice she had called at the house in Josefstrasse, determined to have a bantering quarrel with him—the kind that, in their past relationship, she had known so well how to

turn into love-making. All to no avail. She was beginning to be afraid that, after all, she might have lost
him. So, when he was announced and strode into her
small salon, his dark face set with rage, she decided to
let him suffer a little before she succumbed.

'Well, Anton,' she said coolly, 'have you turned
hermit without your little ward?'

'It is on her account that I am here,' he answered
sharply. 'I sent her to your cousin, believing that she
would be happier amongst young company and that
they would honour my trust and care for her. I particularly informed Graf von Holst, however, that von
Eckerman was to be discouraged, as I told him here,
to his face. I have just seen Eloise and the Gräfin
driving with him in his carriage, which is a shocking
breach of my trust, and while I see the Graf I want you
to impress my views on your cousin.'

Carla smiled. 'But I like Gerhard!'

'You probably do—but you cannot deny that he is a
cheat and a blackguard, living on dishonest money.
Would you allow a daughter of yours to go blindly into
such a liaison?'

Carla raised an eyebrow. 'But Eloise is not your
daughter ... or is she? I have begun to wonder since
you seem so concerned about her!'

Anton clenched his long hands tightly or he might
have slapped her face, and with all his past faults, at
least he had never struck a woman.

'I respected her father greatly, and I take the
responsibility he passed to me very seriously. But I
should have known better than to come to you again
for one last trifling favour, so I will take my leave.' He
turned towards the door.

'Anton!' Carla's tone was so sharp that he paused. 'I

will help you—I was only punishing you a little for that cold emerald necklace when you knew I was expecting *you*. If you will reward me properly this time there is nothing in the world I will not do for you!'

He was shocked at her overt invitation and turned to look at her, his face eloquent with distaste.

'I can accept nothing on those terms. I have never misled you, Carla, never given you any cause to believe there was ever love between us. Pleasant amusement, yes, and on that level it was mutual. But it ended for us both before Eloise even arrived in my house, so understand that you cannot blackmail me with dead ashes!'

Carla sprang up, her cheeks flushed with anger in her turn.

'How *dare* you use such words to me!' she exclaimed. 'I have never begged any man for favours—nor needed to. *If* you can find your emeralds, which are probably behind that cabinet where I flung them, please take them with you—I am no harlot to be paid off with jewels!'

Anton's smile was bitter and sarcastic. 'You used the word—not I. Goodbye, Carla. I apologise for taking up your time.'

He left.

Carla's fury turned to tempestuous tears as she heard him riding away. When she had been his mistress she had felt passion, yes, but no tenderness, merely a greed to attain an acknowledged position in his house and so achieve the heights of her social ambition. Now that he had repudiated her utterly she found that she was desolate from unfulfilled desire for the man himself.

But gradually her devious mind took charge of her

emotions: since Anton had rejected her so brutally she still had it in her power to hurt him far more. No matter what it cost, Gerhard should possess Eloise.

When he called on her later for a glass of wine, Gerhard found Carla pacing her salon impatiently.

'I expected you earlier,' she said excitedly. 'I have such plans, my dear—and they will not fail.'

'As long as they concern Eloise and neither the fat Gräfin nor her silly daughters I am all ears,' he replied pleasantly, pouring two glasses of wine from the decanter on a side table with the familiarity of an old friend. 'I have never paid such a high price for a girl in my life!'

'Not for much longer, Gerhard—I promise you.' Her excitement grew quite feverish. 'In fact I am prepared to martyr myself in your cause!'

Gerhard looked at her more intently—born gossip that he was, he sensed a choice morsel here if he could discover it: 'I take it you have quarrelled with your Count,' he said pleasantly. Carla tossed her head.

'That was a mere bagatelle—Anton and I have our own rules in the game. No, I have been thinking about you, Gerhard, and suddenly seen how simple it can be, for me as well, of course,' she added hastily. 'I can make no move until the wretched Eloise is out of the way—discredited—so I mean to call on her myself, oh, in a most friendly, solicitous way to ask how she fares with my cousin! I will discover which balls, parties or fêtes she is going to attend, while planting secret barbs of my own that will certainly set her against her guardian and almost throw her into your arms. You can easily arrange to be present at one of them and have private words with her about an elopement of some kind—everything is in your favour, since Anton is going to seek out the Graf and blacken your name still further, which is all to your advantage. Then,' she paused dramatically, 'I shall give a party here myself, and invite the von Holsts—and that is the time you must arrange to carry her off.'

Gerhard was frankly puzzled. 'I don't quite follow....'

'Is the girl happy in my cousin's household? Of course not ... and once she knows her guardian can't wait to be rid of her, surely you are the first person she will turn to for help? Oh, you need not commit yourself to marriage or any such nonsense—be all concern and offer to take her anywhere—anywhere in the world she wants to go out of pure kindness!'

Carla sank back on a sofa, the stream of words over, her anger eased for this would be perfect revenge indeed.

Anton was annoyed with himself for appealing to Carla—he should have known better in the light of their past relationship. But fortune was with him. As he rode past one of the city museums on his way back to the stables, he saw the small, dapper figure of Graf von Holst walking down the steps. Anton dismounted and attracted his attention.

'Good afternoon, Mein Graf. You are the very man I want to see!'

The old man looked a trifle nervous. 'I am about to return home, Count Anton, and——'

'This will only take a moment,' Anton smiled—the Graf's nervousness confirmed his suspicions that it was the Gräfin who allowed von Eckerman to see Eloise, and not her husband.

'I caught sight of my ward an hour ago, driving in

the Woods,' he went on. 'She looked very well—but I was puzzled to see that she and your wife were in von Eckerman's carriage. I had hoped you might forbid it?'

His manner was most sympathetic, and the old man sighed.

'I did my best, I promise you, only....' Then he squared his narrow shoulders and met Anton's eyes frankly. 'I am a selfish man, leaving too much on my wife's shoulders,' he went on loyally. 'One cannot expect a woman to turn a man away, so I will see to it myself should it happen again, you have my word on it.'

Anton's smile deepened. He liked the little man and clearly saw his predicament, and admired him for defending his wife. 'Splendid. And it is a great relief to me—for if the man continues to see her I am afraid I may have to remove Eloise and take her back into my own care, and my house is not suited to a young girl at all.'

'Leave it to me, Count!' The Graf hurried into his carriage.

Anton was ashamed of his own amusement but the Graf's face was so transparent; he was obviously far more afraid of having to tell his wife that Eloise might be taken away—thus stopping the most generous payments for her keep—than of standing up to her over von Eckerman. Anton rode on his way, satisfied.

For once the von Holsts had no social engagement for the evening, so the girls had gone out to take coffee with the family next door and the Gräfin and Eloise were just finishing theirs when the Graf came in. His wife raised enquiring eyebrows—he usually went straight to the library.

'Ha! I am glad to find you both together, for I have just met Count Anton.' He turned to Eloise: 'I told you on your first evening here that neither he nor I approved of Herr von Eckerman—and you, too, Gertruda, although you did not listen. Now, unless that man is thoroughly sent about his business, the Count will remove his ward from our house.'

Eloise sprang up furiously. 'But neither of you forbade me his friendship,' she declared. 'And to turn him away tomorrow would be unthinkable—why, he has made special arrangements to take us to the Palace of Schönbrunn and got permission for us to walk through the art gallery, and later to see the gloriette on a hill at the back. Such permission is rare indeed, and you *cannot* hurt his feelings at the last minute!'

'I'm afraid it is necessary, my dear—but you will not be involved, for I shall send him away myself.'

'Oh—and I thought you were my *friend*!'

Beside herself, Eloise rushed out of the room and upstairs. The Gräfin's eyes were bulging with anger for a different reason. Try as she would, she could not take to Eloise—if the girl had wept on her bosom, called her 'Mütti' and placed her girlish hopes and fears in her motherly care—as her own dear girls did—it would have been different. But instead Eloise was a cold fish, dutifully grateful but remote and slightly superior; worse, she turned out to be highly educated and spent much time absorbed in some heavy tomes in the library. At balls and parties she did not even try to impress the younger men so, to the Gräfin, von Eckerman was a gift from heaven, since he obviously adored the little creature. It would have been the perfect answer to get them married off as quickly as possible.

'You are a fool, Hermann,' she told her husband testily. 'You cannot possibly know anything against Herr von Eckerman—and as to her aristocratic guardian, *well*!' she sniffed eloquently. 'He has refused all my invitations, he never attempts to see the girl nor even enquire how she does, so I cannot believe he has much regard for her. Indeed, I suspect he found her as tiresome as I do for I have heard many rumours lately about his own wild life—he and Herr von Eckerman probably fell out over some woman or other, so that the Count's disapproval is nothing more than petty revenge!'

The Graf looked at her large, flushed face for a few moments, then decided that it would be a grave mistake to pass on the still unproved tales of von Eckerman's cheating and dishonesty—she could not be trusted to keep them to herself. Instead he said quietly:

'With all due respect, Gertruda, I think you are wrong. From our conversation when the Count brought Eloise here I think he has a very high regard for her welfare. And what use is it to encourage von Eckerman when we know that no permission will be given for such a marriage?'

'Oh, pouf!' said his wife impatiently. 'I am not interested in keeping the girl here until her marriage. No, once she becomes betrothed—which her guardian cannot forbid, since it is not binding—it will be for Herr von Eckerman to remove her to stay with his own relatives until she comes of age.'

For once she had succeeded in surprising her

husband. 'I thought you were delighted by the money she brings in?'

The Gräfin smiled complacently. 'I must admit it pleased me at first—in fact I have ordered a charming new carriage for my own use. Yours is very serviceable, Hermann, but hardly designed to show off the girls in style! But now that it has become known that we are willing—reluctantly, of course—to take in a girl of good family, I have had many enquiries from my friends. I had no idea that there were so many orphaned nieces and cousins in Vienna! Replacing Eloise with a *far* more pleasant girl will be easy.'

The Graf sighed. He had become very fond of Eloise, even encouraging her to stay on in the library for intelligent conversation if she was still there when he returned for his wine before Mittagessen. He would have given much to have a daughter of his own like her. But, because of that, he must now risk losing her in order to protect her, for von Eckerman would totally destroy her sensitive spirit and lead her a life of misery.

Bracing himself, he said: 'I'm sorry, my dear, but I still feel bound to turn Herr von Eckerman away tomorrow.' And, waiting for no further reaction, he made for the sanctuary of his library.

Eloise was desperate. She too had noticed that Anton never came to call, which could only mean that he was thankful to be rid of her—to return, alone, to his private mourning for his lost great love. As a result she had clung more closely to her only remaining lifelines—the friendship of Gerhard and of the Graf. Now, with one stroke, she was losing them both and the world had become bleak and lonely beyond bearing. She must leave Vienna and go home.

She watched behind the curtains as the Graf dismissed Gerhard the next day. Saw his disbelief, then his sadness followed by reluctant acceptance. After lingering for a moment he entered his carriage and drove away.

Five minutes later a servant knocked on her door to say that the Graf commanded her attendance in the library. Curtly, she refused—pleading yet another mythical headache in excuse. She simply had to be alone to think and make plans.

Since the Gräfin was far from subtle, Eloise was quite aware of her growing dislike of her. Even the girls were less friendly now, finding Eloise unwilling to join in their giggling gossip, which centred endlessly round vapid young men who had or had not flirted with them.

Pacing her room, Eloise decided that the word 'vapid' described her whole life since Anton had brought her here—apart from the very occasional short talks with the Graf, which would now happen no more for she could not forgive him for hurting Gerhard.

Each day her love and longing for Anton deepened. What was the point of prolonging her unhappiness for nearly three more weeks, since she would never find a friend, much less a husband, among the young men she met every evening with the von Holsts? They were presumably grown up, but behaved more like self-conscious fourteen-year-olds.

'I refuse to stay!' she declared out loud, her hands clenched and her beautiful eyes, fiery with rebellion, staring through the window towards the great, free world outside. 'When I reach home and am no longer Anton's ward, then I shall choose my own friends, start building the life *I* want!'

Next day at noon, Eloise was in the library, having refused a half-hearted invitation to go shopping with the Gräfin and her daughters, when a footman announced that the Countess von Schernberg had called and was in the salon. Surprised and reluctant, Eloise went to greet her.

Carla's greeting was effusive—though she was more astonished than ever by Gerhard's obsession with the girl, she seemed so pale and uninteresting.

'My dear Eloise,' she cried, kissing her on both cheeks. 'How fortunate that you are alone! I have come, really, on poor Gerhard's behalf, for he is quite desolate at the treatment he received here yesterday and hopes he hasn't offended you?'

'He most certainly has not,' Eloise replied warmly. She neither liked nor trusted Carla, but any sign of understanding was welcome at this moment. 'It seems that both Graf and Count Anton are determined to break our friendship for reasons I do not know. It is very distressing'.

'Oh, Anton!' Carla gave an indulgent chuckle that implied much. 'Does he visit you here often?'

'Never.' Eloise was unaware of the sadness in her voice, but it did not touch the Countess in the least—merely told her all she needed to know. She leant forward confidingly.

'Listen, my dear—Gerhard is my friend too, and I want to help you both out of this absurd situation. As for Anton—you can leave him to me! The quarrel between those two was always childish—an argument over me, as a matter of fact, when Anton grew jealous of that friendship just as he has over yours. He is so—possessive.' Her little smile was self-satisfied and stung Eloise to the quick: how *could* Anton bear to be intimate with this shallow, hard woman? ... and, obviously, he had gone back to her already. But Carla was hurrying on.

'I have a little plan, Eloise—Anton plans to visit his estate for one night next week, so, when he is away, I shall give a party for you and the von Holsts—and, of course, Gerhard. I will see that you have a chance to talk to him and ease his mind, then we will arrange that you shall meet at my house in future. I warn you, though, you will have to make your peace with him first, for he is quite hurt.'

'Oh, but he must not be!' exclaimed Eloise. 'He has been so kind and thoughtful—he *cannot* think this was ever my doing!'

'Just leave everything to me from now on—you are right to think highly of Gerhard, for he is a great gentleman,' Carla lied, and promptly changed the subject. 'Are you going to many parties at the moment?'

'I believe so,' said Eloise flatly. 'A family called Koch have invited us tonight—I do not know them.'

'Oh, they are delightful, I hear—you may even find Gerhard there!'

'I hope not.' Eloise was upset. 'I shall be forced to refuse to dance with him and then he will be hurt even more!'

Carla stared at her. Had the girl no feminine wiles, no artful techniques at all? 'My dear, there are a dozen ways to convey a message! Your eyes, perhaps, or a small note that can be slipped from your hand to his

unseen ... you don't have to dance with a man
publicly to manage a few words with him in secret!'

Her mission accomplished, Carla rose. 'Do not
mention this visit to Anton if he should call, or our
plan will be ruined. I promise that he will hear nothing
of it from me.'

A few moments later she left, leaving exactly the
impression on Eloise she had intended—that she and
Anton were closer than ever.

Eloise took trouble to look beautiful that evening,
wearing her silver gown and dressing the dark hair
high on her small, shapely head as Serafina's maid had
taught her. She would dearly have liked to call on
Serafina sometimes, but knew that the Gräfin would
insist on coming too, so that talking would be impossible.

Besides, no one—not even the sympathetic
Serafina—could ease her unhappiness now. Only
time and life far from Vienna and Anton could do
that.

For the first time she attracted more hopeful partners than Tina and Lotta von Holst. Smiling, she
allowed her card to be filled and was dancing when
Gerhard arrived, but he was so tall that she saw him
and her heart warmed with affection—how dared
Anton and the von Holsts treat him so badly—and
without reason? She *must* speak to him.

At that moment he saw her and smiled—he had
been well briefed by Carla! He took a partner and
managed to manoeuvre close to Eloise, whose own
partner was laughing uproariously at one of his own
jokes.

Gerhard scarcely moved his lips as he murmured in

Eloise's ear: 'The terrace—end of supper' as he whirled away.

Eloise had already discovered that the ladies' powder closet lay beyond the supper room, in a wide corridor that ended in tall french windows. To slip away would be easy. Her partner for the Supper dance was a young man highly approved by the Gräfin, who thankfully settled herself down to enjoy the rich food with a party of her cronies. Eloise led the way to a table as far from her as possible and forced herself to be enchanting.

When the main course was over and profiteroles covered with thick chocolate and oozing cream were being served, she skilfully managed to flick a speck of cream on her silver gown. Swiftly the young man whipped out his lace handkerchief and tried to dab it away, but Eloise said, 'No, no—I will get the attendant in the powder closet to clean it with warm water. I shall only be a few moments,' and with a dazzling smile she slipped out, sure that he would wait for her.

On the terrace Gerhard was waiting. He seized her arm and drew her to a seat half-hidden by magnolia bushes.

'Eloise—what has happened? I have scarcely slept since the Graf turned me away from the house. What have I done?'

'Dear Gerhard, you have done nothing—and I am as unhappy as you! I would not hurt you for the world, but it seems my guardian has forbidden our friendship. The Countess von Schernberg visited me today, and says it is all because of some silly quarrel he has with you over *her*! Oh, Anton is such a noble, true man—how *can* he sink to pettiness? I could never have believed it of him—never!'

Her great love for him showed plainly in her voice of anguish, and Gerhard smiled to himself in the shadows above her head. So she was in love with the Count! That would make his own conquest of her even sweeter—and more of a challenge. Indeed Carla had done well. Now he must not spoil it by taking Eloise in his arms—not yet. Instead he laid a hand over hers and said gently: 'Of *course* you admired him. But disillusionment was bound to come, dear Eloise. He never wanted you in his house, I'm afraid—I was there when news of your coming arrived and heard him discussing it with Carla. They are very close, you know, and they have resumed their life of pleasure together now that you are safely with the von Holsts.'

He found a strange exquisite pleasure in hurting her, then had to change his cold expression hastily as she turned towards him desperately.

'Oh, Gerhard—help me! You promised you would and I trust you completely—indeed, you are the only person I *do* trust!'

'I will do anything, Eloise. You have only to ask.'

'Then take me away—I promised Anton that I would remain in Vienna for a month, but since he never comes near me and does not seem to care any more, I cannot stand another day in the von Holst household. The Gräfin hates me, the girls are so stupid and now even the Graf has betrayed me.... I have never, never been so wretched in my life.'

'Of course I will rescue you,' he said warmly. 'May I offer you the hospitality of my hunting lodge? It is peaceful and very beautiful.'

'No, Gerhard—I cannot take advantage of your goodness like that, because my affection for you can never become love and I will not hurt you by raising hopes that cannot be. But will you drive me back to my own home in Carinthia? I know that my father's house must be sold, but I have many friends—many places I can stay, and I mean to make my life there. Oh, it is asking a lot of you—it is a long way,' she added anxiously.

'Nonsense,' he chided her gently. 'My carriage is swift and my driver excellent ... nothing done for you can ever be a trouble. Besides, if I may, I shall visit you sometimes in future—just as a friend, I promise!—so I need to know where you will be hiding!'

'How good—how very good you are,' she said gratefully. 'When shall we go?'

Gerhard appeared to think for a few moments, then he said seriously: 'You understand that no one will give permission for such a journey—least of all your guardian?'

'Oh—I had forgot. So I must run away.'

'Yes. Now I will make plans, and I believe there is an ideal opportunity in a few days from now. Carla told me she was intending a party for you——'

'Yes! Within a very few days, she told me today.' Eloise was excited.

'And she will help us, have no fear. When the invitation arrives, here is what you must do. Pack a small valise during the day and find a chance to place it among the bushes by the main gate ... probably when the Gräfin and her daughters are taking a siesta. Then wear your warmest evening gown, for we must drive through the night if we are not to be followed. I will see to it that we slip away long before the party is over, and Carla will make an excuse if your absence is noticed. That should give us a three-hour start at least.

No one will bother by then.'

Eloise raised her head and kissed him on the cheek. 'You have given me hope, Gerhard.'

'Then hurry back to the ballroom now,' he smiled. 'We must not be discovered together out here!'

She sprang up and with only a brief backward smile, ran to the french windows, to find her partner waiting anxiously in the passage:

'You have been gone ten minutes,' he said accusingly.

Laughing, she took his arm. 'I could not resist a little fresh air—you dance so well I declare I was feeling warm, even after supper!'

Beaming, he led her back to the ballroom.

Early the next morning, Gerhard called on a company that hired out carriages of all kinds. He had no intention of using his own when he carried off Eloise—partly because it might be recognised, but more important, he had decided to take a phaeton which he could drive himself. A driver would be a serious embarrassment since the seduction of Eloise must take place long before they reached her own province. A small copse, well off the road where her screams could not be heard, would be ideal if the fine weather held.

He chose an unremarkable phaeton which would not attract attention, hired it for a week and then went on to a public stables to select two fast, reliable horses, to be held ready for collection when he required them.

He smiled to himself as he walked back to his house. His gambler's luck was still running strongly, and his conscience troubled him not at all. In fact he planned to seek out a good card game that evening—a few

thousand schillings in cash might be useful, if Eloise
pleased him and he decided to linger in the country
after all.

He would have laughed had he known that Eloise
went to early Mass that morning, to pray for strength
to make this final break with Anton—and to thank
God most fervently for the staunch, true friendship of
Gerhard, who would never let her down.

CHAPTER
EIGHT

THE invitation from Carla von Schernberg arrived the following morning, for an evening four days hence. The Gräfin was delighted.

'I have often felt a little hurt that after making a good marriage my cousin has bothered so little with us, but now I think she means to make up for it! She moves in *very* high circles, so I am sure we shall meet most interesting people; in fact I feel that all you girls should order new gowns for the occasion!'

Tina and Lotta were excited, but Eloise said: 'I truly do not need one, meine Gräfin—I still have two from Frau Mitzi that I have never worn, and one in particular will be most suitable.'

The Gräfin was annoyed. It had crossed her mind to pass on part of the cost for her daughters' gowns to Count Anton, and that couldn't be done if Eloise refused to have one. But for once, Eloise ignored her expression of displeasure—she was far, far more excited about the invitation than Tina and Lotta: in four days she would be free—and she was hard put to it to keep this joy from showing in her face. Besides, she *did* have the ideal gown for the occasion—a deep cream velvet copied from an Italian painting, with long sleeves and a low, square neckline embroidered with pearls.

'It is a wise choice,' Frau Mitzi had pointed out. 'It is

both chic and unusual and sometimes, even in late spring, the evenings can be very cool.'

Indeed, Eloise thought exultantly, however it started, her evening was going to be *very* cool later on, and she was glad that there was a velvet cape to go with the gown. Gerhard did not appear at the various balls they attended in the meantime, but this did not worry her. He was being prudent and she was grateful for she wanted no more unpleasantness—above all, no report on her to Anton.

The day of Carla's party dawned unduly warm, so that Tina and Lotta were ecstatic when their new gowns, both of fine silk georgette, were delivered—they would be exactly right. Eloise worried a little for the first time. Her heavy velvet, close-fitting at the waist, might cause comment and would, in fact, be highly uncomfortable during the early part of the evening. Then she dismissed such misgivings: she was prepared to endure *any* discomfort since it meant blessed escape. Also, she had much to do before evening.

Packing her small valise was easy—she took only the essentials that she had brought to Vienna with her since she would have no use for the elegant gowns from Frau Mitzi and her familiar, country garments were safely stored in a trunk with her friend Trudi. Instead of going to the library she remained in her room to write the notes of explanation she must leave behind. And the day gradually grew heavier and more humid, with storm clouds gathering on the horizon.

She had written all except the letter to Anton when it was time for Mittagessen and thunder had grown more menacing. It would be a relief if the air cooled before evening, but at the same time she still had to place her valise in the bushes, and if torrential rain poured down during the afternoon it would be hard to explain away her wet day gown should she meet anyone in the house on her return.

The Gräfin was frankly upset by the heat. 'Today of all days!' she wailed, helping herself to a little more of the rich apfelstrudel topped with thick cream. 'It will bring on one of my bilious headaches, I declare, but we must all take a siesta in thin nightgowns immediately, for if we have to send excuses to Carla she may well not invite us again!'

'Oh, Mütti, we *must* go!' cried Lotta.

'I have never had such a beautiful gown,' added Tina.

'Well, I shall *not* be going,' announced the Graf comfortably. 'My presence is not necessary to your enjoyment and I detest this weather.'

No one demurred—least of all Eloise, who was thankful. His sharp eyes watching, as they always did, from his unobtrusive place, were the one thing she had feared. And heaven, she felt, was with her, as the rain had not yet started and, if the others retired soon, she would reach the bushes with her valise before it did.

Indeed, her plan worked perfectly and her spirits rose. When she slipped out of the side door into the garden she did not have to pass the library windows where the Graf had decided to spend the afternoon, and the windows of the Gräfin and the two girls were wide open but closely curtained. By taking a slight detour sheltered by trees and shrubs, Eloise had to cross no open spaces before reaching her goal, and she was safely back indoors within five minutes.

Now all that remained was the letter to Anton.

She moved a small table under her open window, but the heat was oppressive. Partly from that but more certainly from the deep, seething emotions which almost overwhelmed her, Eloise actually felt a slight headache for the first time in her life.

'Dear Anton ...' the words lay flatly on the page, cold, black and expressing nothing of her true feelings. She went to the jug of cold water standing on a marble wash-stand and bathed her forehead with a damp cloth. She must not embarrass him by pouring out her passion, nor reproach him in any way since she understood his indifference ... the same indifference she felt for Gerhard, much as she liked him. No, the note must be brief and factual. She picked up her quill pen and dipped it in the inkwell.

'I cannot ask your forgiveness for breaking my promise, but beg your understanding.' She paused for a while, twirling the quill idly in her hand as she stared out of the window. She wanted, out of gratitude and a sense of justice, to prevent her guardian from disliking Gerhard for such stupid reasons. At last she wrote on:

'Had you visited me I would have told you how impossible I have found it to settle or be happy since leaving your house. And the only person who understood this and is going to help me is the man you have hurt deeply by forbidding our friendship—Gerhard von Eckerman. He is driving me home to Carinthia in his carriage this very night, however, and I hope you will look more kindly on him when he returns, for I shall, at last, be happy.

'I have the address of my father's lawyer and will write to him about money on my arrival, for I wish to take no more from you—you have been so very generous.

'Your affectionate ward, Eloise Reisdorf.'

When she had addressed and sealed the letter, Eloise held it close against her breast as if it could still the ache in her heart, the desperate longing for Anton that made her feel quite ill.

She had planned to leave this beside her letter to the Graf and Gräfin here, on her toilet table, to be discovered early in the morning—or even late tonight. Now she was seized with an irrational idea—suppose she sent it round to his house? When he got in from the stables he would read it and possibly—just *possibly*—come to see her immediately and offer to take her to Carinthia himself!

Love was blinding her to reality, she knew, but how wonderful it would be to share the forty-eight-hour journey in his company—to talk and, perhaps, start her new life with his blessing. The blissful thought grew and grew—even at the risk that he might try to stop her going altogether, for she could persuade him not to do that she felt sure. She had fifty schillings in her purse, for only yesterday the Graf had given her Anton's weekly allowance. Swiftly she took one and went in search of a footman before her impulsive decision could weaken.

She tiptoed downstairs, and good fortune was with her. The youngest footman was just carrying a tray of clean glasses into the dining-room where they would all take wine and sandwiches before setting out—the Gräfin believed this soothed the nerves before a party. He was a pleasant-faced boy and eager to oblige, for he much admired Eloise, and fresh air would be welcome, too.

'You will go straight there?' she insisted, her heart pounding against her ribs.

'With pleasure, Fräulein.' He took the letter, flushing with gratitude as she pushed the schilling into his other hand. Then she was hurrying back to her room, her knees almost too weak to carry her—would he come? Oh, would, *would* he come?

Suddenly she sank from wild elation to despair—of course! Carla had promised to fix the party when Anton was visiting his estate ... he wouldn't even get it! But it was early yet, she thought feverishly, perhaps he had not left....

Then slowly hope died. Her fate was sealed—she would never see him again.

Evening came and still the storm had not broken. Eloise put on her dress at the last moment, the velvet heavy and clinging. She hoped that Gerhard meant them to escape quite early.

As she went downstairs the girls started giggling and the Gräfin exclaimed: 'What can you be thinking of, Eloise? *Velvet*—on a night like this? Go and change immediately—I declare you will swoon in that and ruin the party for us all!'

Her chin up, Eloise said: 'I fear I have a slight chill—I have been shivering these past two hours in spite of the weather, and once the storm breaks the air will freshen.'

The Gräfin sniffed her disapproval—but when they arrived at the Countess's house Carla gave Eloise an almost over-rapturous welcome.

'How lovely you look! I must certainly get Frau Mitzi to make up that same gown for me.' And she kissed the girl on both cheeks. Eloise tried to respond, but a wave of bitter jealousy and dislike made her formal and stilted—tomorrow this woman would be with Anton while she herself would be far away, over the Semmering Pass.

The room soon grew crowded and hot in spite of the wide open french windows, and still Gerhard had not appeared. Eloise found that she *was* shivering—with apprehension. Suppose he did not come at all? That something had happened to him—or that he has changed his mind? Another hour of heat and uncertainty and she most certainly *would* swoon—especially as the company was dull and undistinguished, for Carla had taken little trouble. Her only aim was to cover the elopement of Gerhard and Eloise and to get the girl she hated so deeply out of her life—and Anton's—as quickly as possible.

Then, just as Eloise felt she could stand no more and would have to beg permission to go upstairs and lie down, he arrived, a little flushed with wine now that the object of his desire would be willingly at his mercy so soon. He had collected her valise and the phaeton was waiting discreetly beyond the gates. Nothing could spoil the plan.

He greeted Carla first and her eyes were chilly. As he bent to kiss her hand she whispered harshly: 'You are a fool, Gerhard—the girl won't go if she thinks you are drunk!'

He straightened up. 'But I am not, Carla—and Eloise is far too innocent to realise that I have had a small celebration in advance. Four or five hours' hard driving through the night will clear all trace of wine from my breath before I even touch her!'

'Have you a sword with you?' Carla's voice was pitched low but she was anxious—anxious for the project to succeed for her own sake. 'I will divert the Gräfin as much as possible, but should she raise an alarm when she can no longer see Eloise she might insist on sending a message to Anton. You are not out of the wood yet, my friend!'

'I repeat, I am *not* drunk, and I would not dream of attending your party improperly dressed!' He opened his long, waisted brocade coat and she saw a lethal duelling sword belted in place. 'No one is going to stop me now, Carla, so please smile. Your fierce looks are more likely to rouse suspicion than my innocent stroll through the windows with Eloise . . . she seems in need of air,' he added, looking across the room for the first time and seeing her wan, tense face.

Obediently, Carla produced her fixed, brilliant smile—she was unused to being nervous, but this night's work meant even more to her than to Gerhard, whose lust would soon be satisfied. It was her only chance to wreak revenge and permanent hurt on the man who had spurned her—the only man she now felt hatred for. After tonight Eloise would stand no chance of a good marriage—would be labelled 'harlot' and nothing that Anton could do, with all his popularity and power, would ever restore her to any place in respectable society.

And Gerhard was right—Eloise was so thankful to see him that she attributed his heightened colour to the weather and the same nervous excitement that she felt herself.

'Oh, Gerhard—I was so afraid you would not come!'

'My dear—how could you doubt me? We are sworn friends and I shall never let you down. No, I had to collect your valise, remember, and there were many lights on in the house.'

'Yes, the Graf did not come with us tonight—for which we may be thankful—so the chandeliers will have been lit. Oh, Gerhard, how soon can we leave? I am so hot in this velvet.'

'Stroll gently towards the windows—the Gräfin is absorbed in conversation I see—and I will follow within moments.'

Thankfully she did so, smiling at Tina and Lotta as she passed. They looked petulant, having found no new young men to their liking and wishing that their mother had not built up such high hopes of this 'grand' party. Tina, who was being ogled by a middle-aged man, cried: 'Come and join us, Eloise!'

But Eloise, fear squeezing her heart now, said: 'No—you were right about my dress. It is too heavy, and I must have a little fresh air.'

'Oh, we will come too,' offered Lotta eagerly.

Eloise panicked. If they came with her all would be ruined, and half the party would soon crowd the cooler garden outside. Then Gerhard, a glass of champagne in his hand, came to the rescue. With his most charming, conspiratorial smile he whispered to Tina and Lotta: 'Give us ten minutes alone, I beg you—you know how unjustly your parents frown on me!'

And, leaving the girls intrigued at this romantic turn in a dreary evening, he guided Eloise outside.

'Oh, Gerhard, let us go now—*now*! I am so frightened,' she implored.

He drained his champagne—a mistake after a litre of strong red wine, but he was feeling elated and triumphant. Eloise looked virginal as a bride in the cream velvet, the lines emphasising her tiny waist and young, firm breasts—but she mustn't look so anxious, he thought.

'Come, smile for me while I can see you,' he said lightly. 'We are off on a great adventure—taking you to freedom, not going into mourning!'

He was so full of gaiety, his own smile so infectious that slowly she responded, at first looking up tantalisingly under her long lashes then opening her eyes wide with a sparkle of excitement. Satisfied, he caught her hand and led the way out of the circle of light and round to the drive, keeping on the grass verge.

When they reached the street Eloise said: 'But where is your carriage, Gerhard?'

He laughed softly. 'You promised to trust me, Eloise, and I'm taking no risks of having you snatched away. No, this phaeton will go like the wind and no followers will catch up with us. Let me lift you up.'

His hands closed tightly round her waist—hot and oddly possessive. She remembered how coarse they were and a tremor of fear went through her. What did she really know of this man? Suppose Anton and the Graf were right after all? Swiftly she said: 'My cape! I must go back and fetch it!'

But Gerhard only laughed again, swung her up, and sprang into the driving seat.

'I brought one for you, never fear.' He whipped up the horses as he added: 'I have been to too much trouble to chance this journey being spoilt now.'

And they were off into the darkened city, the phaeton lurching a little so that Eloise had to hold tightly to the handrail beside her seat and wished, in spite of the heat, that they were in a closed carriage with a driver.

She tried to dismiss the apprehension prickling up her spine—after all this was *Gerhard*, her trusted friend—only she had never known him in such a reckless mood before. Admittedly, she knew he was in love with her, but his courtesy and consideration had let her push that knowledge to the back of her mind.

Now he was driving as though this long journey was some kind of triumph instead of an unselfish wish to help her. Besides, although he'd said he had brought a cloak for her he had forgotten to give it to her. Suddenly she wanted the phaeton to stop—to get out while they were still inside Vienna so that they could talk as they used to, and he could still her ridiculous fears.

'Gerhard—may I have the cloak you brought? At this speed the air is quite sharp.'

Surely he would have to pull up in order to hand it to her. Instead he flicked the horses to a faster pace.

'Wait until we are clear of the city, my dear,' he said loudly. 'I am as nervous as you are. If your absence is discovered we may be hotly pursued, and I have no wish to be defeated now! You shall have the cloak when we are out on the open plains—there we shall be safe.'

Safe! she thought wildly, as the phaeton lurched round a corner far too fast, balanced briefly on two wheels and the horses already lathering. The Graf's serious, intelligent face swam before her eyes—then Anton, enforcing his embargo on this friendship so positively. Oh, why had she been so young and foolish—so certain that her own judgement of Gerhard was the right one?

She stole a look at his profile as they passed a lighted house in the suburbs—one of the last they might see—and knew that her fears were true. She could almost have wished that a carriage would career round the next corner to crash into them and cause a halt. The injuries to everyone would be terrible, even fatal, but anything would be preferable to this. Only there were no vehicles abroad at this time—carriage folk were either safe at home or attending functions that would not end for two hours at least.

Gerhard's profile was that of a stranger—the sensuous lips a little slack as the night air heightened the effects of the wine he had drunk; the wide, candid blue eyes now mere slits as the rocking phaeton gathered still more momentum.

'Oh, Gerhard—please *stop*!' she cried, catching his arm.

He shook off her hand: 'Careful, Eloise, or you will cause a spill! You are not afraid, are you? I thought you were different from most women—that you would dare anything for your freedom.' His tone was jeering.

She clenched both her hands over the rail to steady herself.

'It is not my escape but your demon driving that frightens me, Gerhard,' she retorted with spirit. 'You must be ill to take such risks—I would rather hold the reins myself!'

He burst out laughing: 'What? A tiny creature like you handling two mettlesome horses? They will quieten when we are beyond the city and then we will go at funereal pace if you wish.'

Soon the last houses were behind them, and ahead

stretched the wide, flat plains, the darkness thicker and more menacing in the far distance where the Northern Alps began to rise. A warning flicker or two of lightning already played over them spasmodically, although the distance was too great for thunder to be heard.

Gerhard didn't slacken speed as he had promised and Eloise shivered. *Had* Anton got her letter by some miracle? She knew that his estate was this side of Semmering, so was it possible that he might be waiting to waylay them?

But her letter was lying unopened in the hall at Josefstrasse, since Anton had met an old friend—his rival in the trotting races—and they had gone to dine at a famous Weinstube to pass a few hours companionably talking of horses and the coming racing season.

However Eloise knew nothing of this and, holding fast to the hope that he was waiting somewhere ahead, she forced her fear to the back of her mind and began to think furiously. First she tried to ask once more. 'Gerhard—you promised me the cloak when we reached the Plain—I need it now.'

'There are pleasanter ways to get warm, beautiful Eloise,' he chuckled, and transferring both reins to one hand he reached out to draw her against him with the other. She shrank away as far as she dared without actually falling out of the light phaeton and, with a sharp curse, his hand could barely reach her arm without making him overbalance.

But now she knew for certain that Gerhard was either run mad or drunk. Far from being a gentle, charming partner and a friend whose cause she had obstinately supported against all wise advice, he was evil. Because she knew little about sex in spite of her country upbringing, rape mercifully did not cross her mind, but that he intended something unpleasant was obvious.

The only crumb of comfort was that by transferring the reins awkwardly to his right hand he had got them tangled and this slowed their headlong pace as the horses, almost as frightened as she was, felt a slackening and began to toss their heads wildly and attempted to rear in protest.

Gerhard's curses were voluble now as he swayed a little in his seat, striving to regain control.

'You are not well, Gerhard,' Eloise said firmly when he paused for breath. 'I insist that we spend the night at an inn a little farther on. My aunt and I passed it on our journey to Vienna and we shall be quite safe from any pursuers. No one will recognise this phaeton, as you said, and by morning you will be better and the storm will have passed.'

'Not *well*? I have never felt better or happier in my life,' he retorted. 'I have promised to take you over the Alps and I mean to do so. We are barely five leagues from Vienna yet.'

So I shall have to jump, Eloise thought desperately, for to continue this nightmare drive was unthinkable. Besides, the first rumbles of thunder were audible and she knew that the storms of Austria were dreaded for their violence over mountains—the peaks attracted and held the lightning and caused the thunder to reverberate with twice its usual ferocity and clamour. To face that, with a madman beside her, made the risk of hurting herself in a fall negligible.

She must wait, though, until the inn was at least in sight. There would be friendly people there, and help if Gerhard should come looking for her....

It was the custom for all inns to keep a lantern burning outside all through the night to guide weary travellers or those whose horses had gone lame. And less than a league further on and far closer than she remembered, Eloise saw the little glow in the distance—more welcome and more beautiful than any star. From that moment she concentrated on the verge of the road, waiting and praying for a stretch of thick grass to break her fall.

Luckily the horses were travelling much more slowly now. Gerhard had regained control but even vicious flicks of his whip would not spur them on—they were not trained for either speed or long journeys, being merely hired hacks whose usual task was to pull worthy Burghers round Vienna at a sedate pace with frequent stops for sight-seeing or business calls. By now they were weary and short-winded.

Her eyes used to the darkness now, and helped by the flashes of livid light from the storm ahead, Eloise saw, at last, a likely spot coming nearer....

Deeply thankful for her early training as a climber, she shifted her grip on the hand-rail and turned her body carefully into a position that would give her most leverage when she sprang—for Gerhard would give her no second chance if she failed, of that she was certain.

But her movements, cautious though they were, attracted his attention and, after her cringing away from his earlier grasp, he instantly guessed her purpose. Sharply he reined in the horses to a halt so sudden that she was thrown forward with a gasp. Before she had recovered her balance Gerhard was holding her arm in a vice-like grip.

'Escape, would you?' he said through clenched teeth. 'You who have tormented me with those great eyes ever since we met, who were so glad to see me on every social occasion and accepted my proffered love without a protest because it suited you! Then you beg me to "rescue" you—regardless of the dangers it lays me open to on my return to Vienna! For all your beauty you are a monster, Eloise—am I supposed to serve you meekly with no reward at all? Oh, no! I am a man and will claim my dues!'

His face was close to hers—at last she smelt the wine on his breath, and a flash of lightning showed his blue eyes glittering with venom and desire.

'You are drunk, Gerhard,' she said coldly, although her body was shivering again and fear beat against her brain. 'You shall be rewarded, I promise—but not when you are in this state. If you drive on quietly and steadily—otherwise the horses may drop dead from exhaustion—we will complete our journey to my home and then, when you are sober, discuss things quietly as we always used to do.'

He was quivering at her nearness, the sweet scent of her hair, but befuddled still as he was, he knew that this was not the place for his purposes, not with that wretched inn within sight.

'Very well—but first I shall give you a taste of what to expect, what you must have known I should demand!' And, before she could turn her head away, his lips closed down over hers, harsh and cruel, forcing her mouth open.

It was an hour and a half after Gerhard had set off with Eloise that Anton returned home—his dining companion had refused to stay out late in case his wife grew anxious.

As soon as Anton saw the envelope addressed to him in Eloise's hand, he dashed back to the door and called to his driver to wait: she must be in some trouble to send him a letter.

He ripped open the envelope and drew out the single half-sheet of paper, his eyes darkening with horror as he read the message.

Fortunately he was still in his riding-habit so, pausing only long enough to take down his duelling sword from the wall—unused for many years but always kept polished and sharpened—he buckled it on and rushed to the carriage, shouting as he leapt in, 'To the stables—and drive for your life!'

His only chance of catching the runaways lay with Leo—no carriage, not even the light equipage he used for racing, could hope to overtake another vehicle. Besides, he had no idea when they had started. All he knew, with blinding clarity at last, was that Eloise was his one and only love—the most precious thing in the world—and that her note, although so formal, had been a muted cry for help.

He burst into the stables, waking the watchman into startled consciousness.

'Quickly, man—my saddle and bridle for Leo,' he commanded as he strode to the stall and led the stallion out. His mind was ice-clear and he blessed the position of his own estate, for from long experience he knew many short cuts across country which, if God was with him, would cut several leagues off the journey to Semmering made by a carriage.

In a matter of seconds Leo was saddled and Anton sprang into it, riding like the wind straight out of the open door and into the street.

'Go, Leo—go as you have never gone before!' he called to the horse who, used to great speed and enjoying long distances, responded immediately. Man and horse were as one—but could they possibly be in time?

CHAPTER
NINE

FIGHTING back nausea, Eloise sat shocked and still, her hands over her bruised lips and the stench of stale wine reeking in her nostrils. Escape was impossible now since Gerhard, turned sullen by her revulsion and utter lack of response to his experienced kissing, had made her a prisoner. Angrily he had fumbled for the cloak in the back of the phaeton, but instead of placing it round her shoulders he knotted it firmly round her waist, holding the ends round the reins in his hands.

'You little fool,' he mumbled, 'I meant to woo and win you, but I swear it will go hard with you now!'

In the darkness, with his mind clouded, he had forgotten her delicate beauty, the pure virginity which had even made him consider marriage at one point. Now she had become an object for savage revenge—a woman who had spurned him after all his efforts to please her. He sank into maudlin self-pity. In two hours at most they should reach the spot selected in his mind as ideal; since she was behaving so stupidly he would carry her there when he stopped the phaeton, and after that she could not possibly escape. He no longer wished to please her by his love-making, to make her respond gladly—no, he would ravage her for his own satisfaction, and if it killed her, he did not care. Nobody would ever find her body and, if they did, no harm could come to him. Aristocrats were never indicted for serious offences, apart from treason.

He felt better as he thought of the secret place he had discovered high in the mountains soon after he won the hunting lodge at cards. It lay well off the road, and he felt sure that Eloise's screams would not be heard—even if any traveller was foolish enough to be abroad during such a storm which, as they drove on, grew louder and louder. Soon huge drops of rain began to fall, singly at first, bouncing against the hood, then increasing to a downpour which curtained off everything round them.

Glancing helplessly over her shoulder, Eloise saw the lantern outside the inn, behind them now, slowly blotted out, and she knew that all hope of rescue was gone. There was nothing now except lightning made more dazzling by the rain and claps of thunder that seemed to crack the sky itself. Gerhard's face showed grim in the flashes of light, and her left shoulder and side of her gown were drenched by the driving rain.

A strange calm came to her and she began, silently, to pray. She was quite certain she was going to die, if not at Gerhard's hand then through an accident, for the horses were terrified by the storm and stumbled and slithered on the streaming road as it began the slow ascent up the mountain. She closed her eyes and let thoughts of Anton fill her mind—at least she would not die unfulfilled since she had experienced perfect, overwhelming love—a love that could never come again if she lived to be an old woman.

His beloved, dark face seemed very near, the eyes amused and tender as they had been during their rare talks together—she dared not think of his long, strong hands because they renewed her horror of Gerhard's coarse ones. But memory of his kisses would not be denied—their sweet passion which had seemed to draw the very soul from her body in yearning.

Softly, unaware that she spoke aloud, she cried his name. 'Anton—oh, *Anton*!'

'You'll never see *him* again, that's very sure,' Gerhard scoffed loudly above the storm. 'If Carla can't have him you may be certain nobody else will be allowed to ... besides, he won't want you after this escapade! No, not even as his ward.'

But Eloise was alert, her dreams forgotten.

'What do you mean "If Carla can't have him"? She has him already—she told me so, and you confirmed it!'

Gerhard laughed. 'What a foolish little thing you are, Eloise—quite pitifully easy to gull! Do you honestly believe that Carla would have gone to all the trouble of giving that party tonight—of helping us to escape—if she really had your precious Count in her grasp? No, she needn't have bothered. It is because he has spurned her that she was so anxious to help—to hurt him by helping to disgrace *you*.'

'Oh, no!' exclaimed Eloise, sitting upright, her eyes wide with anguish. 'Death will be a merciful punishment if I have truly been the instrument to harm him!' And tears came, bitter and agonised. 'I only wish he could know how deeply I regret this—regret *everything....*'

'Well, he never will know, will he?' taunted Gerhard. 'No one is pursuing us—nor likely to in this weather!'

Anton and Leo covered the ground, blended together like a single, powerfully moving statue, both drenched black by the heavy rain, but Leo never faltered.

They had galloped over rough fields, jumped hedges and ditches, and as they drew nearer to the violence of the storm Anton crouched low on the stallion's neck, soothing him in the quiet authoritative voice the horse knew so well.

'We are going to find her, Leo,' he insisted. 'What is a storm to us? Thunder and lightning cannot harm you—we have weathered many a storm before this. Come on, boy—come on. . . .'

At last they joined the road where it began to climb upward to Semmering. With all his heart Anton thanked God that at least Eloise had told him their destination for there was no other way to reach it but this. He doubted, too, whether Gerhard would show his hand before reaching the mountains where there were many caves and great boulders to offer shelter, for he would not dare molest her in front of his driver.

Suddenly Leo, like the tired horses ahead of him, began to slither on the loose stones of the road, now rapidly turning into an angry stream as the rain pelted down. Cursing silently, Anton was forced to slow their pace; if Leo went lame or damaged his legs in any way, it would take an hour at least to scale the mountain on foot.

'It's all right, Leo—steady now, take it easy.'

Anton looked upwards desperately, trying to see if anything was moving above them, for the road curved up the side of the mountain towards the Pass. A great flash of lightning, brighter than any before, rewarded him at last. Far ahead a black shape, distorted by the rain, was moving slowly, and his heart leapt. It *must* be them, for no ordinary traveller would venture this way on such a night.

He dared not urge Leo to go faster, much as he ached to do so, but they were in such harmony that the stallion caught something of his excitement and, of his own accord, went carefully into a trot, his feet feeling their way as delicately as a dancer.

'Oh God,' Anton prayed fervently, 'let me be in time ... in time....'

At that moment, Leo lost his footing.

Eloise had stopped weeping, drained of all emotion. Instead she was determined to meet whatever Fate had in store with courage—a courage that Anton would have been proud of, even though he would never hear of it.

Meantime the cold, rain-drenched air had cleared Gerhard's head at last and he was no longer drunk, only possessed once more with excitement. The cave was not far off now and the raging thunder and lightning seemed fitting music for the coming scene he planned.

'We will shelter in a few minutes,' he told Eloise, and her heart sank. The elation in his voice told her very clearly that, whatever he intended, she had almost run out of time.

'Aren't you glad?' he insisted.

'I would prefer to travel on.'

'What? and kill the horses? They must have rest.'

'Then why did you refuse to stop at the inn?' she asked coldly. 'We could all have rested then. What drives you on like this, Gerhard? You are not the man I thought I knew at all.' She felt so completely detached now that this really interested her.

He laughed. 'Would you have entrusted yourself to me if you *had* really known me?' He parried with another question.

'No.'

'But I had to possess you, you see—you have sent me mad ever since I first saw you, and you seemed far from unwilling. Then your wretched guardian interfered—even succeeded in setting that stupid Gräfin against me—and I could not wait for three long years, because the image of you came between me and everything else in my life. So—this was the only way.'

'Are you planning to marry me, then—somewhere in secret?'

He turned to stare at her, intrigued by this new mood after all her emotion. But she stared straight ahead, her damp hair plastered to her beautiful skull in close, black tendrils—wet and dishevelled he found her more attractive than ever and he tried to lash the horses to greater speed but the road grew steadily steeper and they could make no more effort.

'Well—are you?' she repeated.

'No. That would have been a last resort and marriage would never suit me.'

She could scarcely believe such bland egotism—it did, indeed, amount to a form of madness. However, all she said was: 'How much strain it must have caused you to be so very charming.'

'Not at all,' he said blithely. 'I knew all the time that I was working exactly to this end—in fact it had come about more quickly than I dared to hope, and being tantalised merely deepened my sense of coming pleasure!'

'You are the one who should be called "Satan",' she said in the same cool voice. 'For you really *are* a devil incarnate.'

'Hate and love are very close together, Eloise—and you will come to love me before this night is over,' he said complacently.

At that she did turn to look at him and a flash of lightning showed him such a burning hatred in her eyes that for a moment he flinched.

'If I can I shall gladly kill you—for I swear you will never possess me! I don't mind if I die myself in the attempt, since you and your vile Carla have seen to it that I have no hope left in life anyway.'

They went on in silence, Gerhard's mind working furiously, for, remembering the proud set of her head and the firm little chin, he was in no doubt that she meant exactly what she said. He must keep her securely tied by the cloak and, on reaching the cave, find some means of slipping off and hiding his sword, since it was the only weapon she might discover. Besides, he would not be needing it to fight Anton now—they had got clean away without any pursuit.

It took a long, long half-hour to reach the pass, the journey made more hazardous by loose stones and small boulders that came clattering down the mountain side on to the road, driven by the force of the storm and rain which had in no way abated.

But at last they arrived at his chosen spot and he guided the phaeton just off the road to a patch of rough scrub, partly shielded by an outcrop of rock so large that no storm would ever shift it.

'I will carry you the rest of the way,' he said, pulling on the brake which locked the back wheels.

But Eloise seized the chance while his hands were occupied. Whipping the ends of her cloak from the reins, since Gerhard had only looped them round, she jumped out, her legs so numbed with cold that she staggered helplessly at first on the uneven ground.

She knew Gerhard would be after her within seconds but, momentarily, the thunder and lightning were only grumbling and flickering fitfully as they regathered their strength.

'Oh God—dear Lord—let me find hiding before he can see me!' She prayed aloud, half-sobbing as she forced her painful legs to obey her—the slow return of her circulation made them an agony, and her feet were soon on loose shale which slithered down behind each step in what seemed to be a deafening clamour. He could follow the sound and find her so easily ... but desperation made her stumble on and upward without even glancing over her shoulder.

It was so dark! She could see nothing through the rain but, bending almost double, she used her hands to feel the way ahead and suddenly they felt a fissure in the rock looming beside her. It was only a narrow cleft, reaching inwards scarcely a matter of inches, but she crushed herself inside, ignoring the grazing and bruising of her arms and shoulders if only she might be hidden. ...

Then a renewed flash of brilliant lightning showed her two things—Gerhard barely four steps away, and the cloak! Her frantic scrambling had unravelled the roughly tied knot round her waist and it must have fallen to the ground unnoticed as she squeezed into the small opening.

And in the same flash of light, Gerhard saw it too ... and saw her just beyond. His face was livid with rage and rain streamed over him, bedraggling his fair hair forward over his ears and down to his shoulders. She shuddered. He looked like a wild beast of prey rather than anything human. Then, as a great peal of thunder burst overhead he reached out and caught hold of her.

'Escape, would you?' he snarled. 'Oh no, my pretty—not after all I've been through to get you here!' And he dragged her towards him, throwing her over his shoulder as though she were no more than a sack. With bleeding hands, cut against the rock as he pulled her out so roughly, she beat feebly against his back, but all strength had gone out in that one desperate bid for safety.

His progress was slow and uncertain as the loose stones shifted under each step and two or three times he half-fell, but Eloise was hardly aware of it. Pain seemed to break over her body in waves from head to foot. At some point she must have twisted an ankle, her knees were grazed and her arms and shoulders began to throb from the rough embrace of the rock fissure. Her head throbbed, too, with hanging downwards over Gerhard's shoulder, and she shut her eyes, wishing passionately that death would come now, this moment, and bring blessed relief from this appalling, pain-filled nightmare before they reached their destination where a far worse torture awaited her.

Gerhard stumbled on in grim determination. He, too, was numbed and grazed and his head ached from a mixture of blinding anger and a hangover from the earlier excess of wine. But nothing—nothing on heaven or earth was going to stop him now. His feelings were chaotic—he no longer desired Eloise as the exquisitely tantalising girl he had known in Vienna, instead she had become some sort of primeval goddess, malevolent, the cause of all this night's traumatic events, and he must destroy her. Destroy her first with his own body so that no unappeased desire could return later to torment him, then leave her abandoned in the cold cave to whatever fate awaited her. And they were nearly there. . . .

He felt that he had been climbing the slippery slope for ever, yet he knew that, in reality his secret place was a scant two hundred paces above the road—only this violent night had killed any sort of reality and turned it into a test of endurance.

At last he stood in the mouth of the cave, breathless, his head swimming a little. Sensing the sudden stillness of motion and a danker atmosphere, Eloise opened her eyes but could see nothing. Although she was such a slight weight Gerhard heaved her off his shoulder awkwardly so that she found no footing and fell backwards, her head mercifully missing a jagged stone, but her shoulders suffered more bruises. Her velvet evening slippers had long since torn to ribbons, and now the remnants fell off entirely.

For a full minute time was suspended, the man breathing so harshly that it could be heard above the rain and the girl partly stunned, waiting. Then Gerhard remembered his sword—it must be hidden while they were both blinded by the deeper darkness of this shelter. His hand fumbling, he unbuckled the belt and feeling with his other for some small concealing boulder, he found one and dropped belt and sword behind it. His headache eased with the cessation of effort and he made a mental note of the position of the boulder in relation to the cave's entrance—he must not leave without being armed.

The cave was not large but high enough for a tall man to stand upright, and a little farther back the ground was smooth and still fairly dry. With his body blocking the entrance there was no chance for Eloise to slip out—besides, one of her feet still lay against his ankle, so she had not moved. As his breath slowly steadied he bent down and groped for her body to carry it on to the smoother surface.

Under his loathsome hands she held herself limp, hoping he would think her unconscious and leave her alone for a while to recover before making his attack. Then, hopelessly, she stiffened and raised her head—what was the use of prolonging all this?

For the last time she asked faintly: 'Will you not spare me, Gerhard? To save your own soul, will you not let me go without further harm?'

'No,' he replied violently. 'You yourself have described me as the devil—what soul have I to save? Come, take off this sodden mess,' and he pulled at her gown, but the thick velvet resisted his cold hand. 'Take it *off*,' he commanded, and with frightened, icy fingers she fumbled at the tiny embroidered buttons and loops swollen with the rain. Sadly, all her courage had suddenly deserted her when she needed it most—she was shaking with terror now that the awful, final moments had arrived.

Gerhard grew impatient and reached for her, drawing her hard against him. Forcing back her head he began to kiss her until she was half swooning from the ferocious impact.

Suddenly, unbelievably, she heard her name being called against the storm. Perhaps this was dying, for no one could possibly be out there searching for her. Then, unmistakably, it came again.

'*El-o-ise*.'

Jerking her head aside sharply she summoned all her remaining breath and screamed—screamed until the walls of the cave echoed with the sound. Gerhard was so startled that it was seconds before he clamped a hand over her mouth. His blood was pounding so fiercely in his ears with renewed passion that he had not heard the voice from outside.

'It is useless to make that noise,' he shouted in her ear. 'No one is within miles of this place and well you know it.'

'Aren't they?' The voice slashed the air in its anger and as Gerhard swung round a sheet of lightning showed Anton, his sword drawn, standing in the mouth of the cave.

'Oh, Anton!' gasped Eloise as she sank, quite spent, to the ground.

'Draw your sword, von Eckerman—although you deserve to be killed like the dog you are!'

'I am unarmed,' Gerhard's voice shook for it was his turn, at last, to know fear, and physically he had always been a coward.

In spite of her exhaustion Eloise cried: 'It's not true. He was wearing a sword on the drive ... I felt it.'

Anton took a step forward. 'The time for your trickery is past—unsheathe at once or I shall run you through the heart.'

'Give me time—I—I dropped it off near the entrance to this cave. I must find it, I *must*.' The swaggering bully had become a gibbering supplicant, edging forward and scrabbling ahead of him as his hands searched for the boulder. He was a passable swordsman, but Anton von Arnheim was famed as the finest in all Austria.

'I meant no harm,' he pleaded as his search went on and Anton remained sternly silent. 'We—we had to shelter from the storm ...'

A sob from Eloise was more eloquent than any words. Relief and utter thankfulness overwhelmed her and her tears flowed.

A clatter of metal proclaimed that Gerhard had found his weapon.

'Come outside,' commanded Anton, stepping between him and Eloise, kneeling somewhere in the darkness of the cave. 'And you go first, von Eckerman—I do not trust you an inch.'

As she heard steel striking steel Eloise dragged herself forward—her anxiety for Anton was so great that she must see what was happening. The storm had, at last, rolled away into the distance, taking the heavy clouds with it, so that the sky was suddenly clear and stars appeared so that both men were visible.

Anton was the better swordsman but von Eckerman was desperate, fighting for his very life. Although the ledge of ground outside the cave was almost flat it was still slippery, and hampered both swordsmen as it was difficult to gain a firm foothold.

Eloise crouched in the mouth of the cave, her painful hand clasped in prayer, her eyes never leaving Anton for a second. He must win ... he *must*....

But at first the fight was perilously even. Gerhard was powerfully built and each thrust and parry carried great weight behind it, forcing Anton to slither backwards more than once. Then, with a shout of triumph, Gerhard drew blood and Eloise gasped—the thin sleeve of Anton's riding shirt, plastered as close to his flesh as a second skin now, ripped, and blood began to flow.

'Ha, von Arnheim,' crowed Gerhard, 'you are not as mighty as your reputation!'

But his pride cost him dear, for momentarily he was off guard and Anton's rapier laid open his shoulder. It was a fierce thrust, and Gerhard dropped his sword as his arm sagged.

'Pick it up!' Anton ordered sharply.

With blood slowly oozing down his chest Gerhard stooped, and in stooping caught sight of Eloise, though he gave no sign and she did not notice since her eyes were never on him. But why, oh why, she thought frantically, did Anton not strike his opponent down then and there, when the advantage was all his and Gerhard so much deserved to die? His next words gave her the answer.

'Do not play for time, von Eckerman—on guard! Even a swine like you I will not kill in cold blood—*fight*!'

The blood was dropping down on to his hand, now, and Gerhard was afraid—how deep *was* his wound? And what chance had he of mercy, much less tending, from the ruthless man opposite? Suppose the strength was draining steadily from his sword-arm, von Arnheim would not have to kill in cold blood—he could and would leave him alone on this desolate mountain to bleed to death.

Anton's blood was flowing more freely too, and Eloise ached to run out and staunch it, but knew she must not make the slightest move to distract him. Only Anton himself knew that the cut was quite superficial, and it worried him not at all.

Fear renewed von Eckerman's strength and he lunged forward quite suddenly, to find Anton's weapon ready to thrust his harmlessly upwards and, in less than a second, score the blade swiftly down his unprotected side in a long, thin cut that burned, although it was not deep.

Eloise closed her eyes for the first time. The tension was unbearable and the crouching position increased her own physical pains intensely, yet she dared not move even an inch to ease them. There was another echoing clash and her eyes flew open as, with horror, she saw Gerhard thrust low, then in the nick of time Anton stepped sideways so that the thrust met thin air and the force he had put into it brought him to his knees.

'This is the second chance I have given you—now fight fairly, for it will be the last,' Anton's voice was harsh and cutting in its utter contempt. Gerhard staggered to his feet for the second time, but now he was inflamed with the rage of an injured bull, and, as the full moon sailed out from behind the last of the clouds, bathing the ghastly scene in silver light, he charged blindly at his enemy.

Again, Eloise closed her eyes—could Anton possibly defend himself from the savagery of a man possessed? A sudden clatter of steel on stone forced her to look again. There, barely two paces from where she was, lay a rapier—was it Anton's? In dread she compelled herself to look upwards, and surprise and thankfulness filled her.

The two men were standing quite close to her, their faces plain to see in the moonlight. It was Gerhard who had been disarmed while Anton had the point of his sword held against the other's breast.

'You have lost, von Eckerman,' he said sternly, 'and I am now at liberty to kill you as honour permits and, God knows, the world will be a cleaner place for your passing. But first I order you to confess—even a rat has that right, although I am no priest to shrive you'.

Gerhard's eyes were bloodshot as his fear and madness mounted. His hand was scrabbling the air, trying vainly to reach and somehow staunch his bleeding wounds.

'I will do nothing at your bidding, von Arnheim—*nothing*,' he snarled, his lips drawn back like an animal's at bay.

'You have no choice.' Anton pressed the point a little harder to make this quite clear. 'Now, down on your knees—no, a little farther back where Fräulein Reisdorf can hear your voice clearly.'

It was the first time that Eloise was certain that he had seen her all along and she was glad, although she shrank instinctively as Gerhard was driven so close to her she could hear his hard breathing and almost smell his fear. Then he slowly sank to his knees where he could make no sudden movement away from the sword that was threatening him.

'Now—*confess*,' repeated Anton shortly. 'Did you not become rich by robbing and cheating innocent and gullible men in Vienna? Cheating, above all, at every card game you were allowed to join?'

Eloise looked up at his stern face in astonishment—why was this confession necessary at such a moment? Or had Anton, too, lost his mind? In his state of pain and fury, every moment that von Eckerman lived he could still be a mortal danger. But the violence of Gerhard's cursing half under his breath told her that the purpose of this was all too serious—it had to be done.

'Make haste—delay will not serve you now,' insisted Anton.

'Damn your soul to hell, von Arnheim!' Gerhard's voice was ragged, 'I admit nothing.'

'I insist. Are you not a cheat?'

The answer was an indistinct mumble, so Anton went on: 'I shall find all the evidence I need amongst your effects, but it is vital to me that Fräulein Reisdorf shall hear of your villainy from your own lips—that she will understand why I intend to repay all your victims as soon as possible. Was the hunting lodge to which you planned to take her won from a worthy old man because you used marked cards against him?'

'Yes.' The word was bitten off like a curse.

Now Eloise understood the desperate need behind what Anton was doing—just as he had ridden through the storm to save her, his ward, so he needed these facts to save many, many more innocent victims of von Eckerman in the past. But she was frightened. The kneeling man was like a clenched threat of murderous anger every moment that he remained alive—and he was strong, as she knew only too well.

Then a final question from Anton, edged with pure hatred, caught her attention and made her gasp.

'You have ruined so many—but your most dastardly act of all was to set out deliberately to rape Fräulein Reisdorf by feigning friendship for her, was it not? Knowing that your selfish pleasure would reduce her to the wretched life of a harlot—that under the strict conventions in Austria she could have no future hope of marriage—even to me, who love her with my whole being!'

'Anton!' Eloise forgot everything in the miracle of his words and, such was the ordeal they had both been through, he made the one grave mistake of letting his eyes meet hers in a look that conveyed his burning love and compassion for what she had suffered.

At that point Gerhard was indeed insane, and with the craftiness of a madman who had nothing left to lose, he groped stealthily for his sword, his hand moving so swiftly and silently that the other two, locked in a brief moment of mutual joy and discovery, were unaware of it—especially as Anton's sword was still so firmly placed against its target.

With his rapier in his left hand Gerhard turned his body towards Eloise with such a sharp jerk that it threw Anton's direct aim off-balance.

'You shall *never* have her!' he shrieked, as the blade flashed through the air.

Eloise opened her eyes still wider in astonishment as she felt a sharp blow somewhere beneath her ribs. Apart from the shock she felt no immediate pain but she automatically pressed her hands to her side to find a slow, hot warmth flowing out over them.

She felt her body sagging backwards and a slow film was spreading over her sight. 'Oh, Anton, my dearest love, he has killed me!'

Just before she lapsed into merciful unsconsciousness she heard Anton's voice, sharper than any steel. 'To hell with you and your evil soul, von Eckerman—this is an execution.'

There was a muted scream close by—then silence. Eloise knew no more.

ELOISE felt dimly that she was floating in blackness; she could hear faint, far sounds above her and yet she seemed to have no body—to be weightless. But the sounds were drawing her—calling to her, although they had no words that she could distinguish.

With a great effort she began to float towards them in long, slow spirals and the blackness grew less dense. She was conscious of pain somewhere, and yet she had no body and her ears were muffled. Then, as she spiralled higher, she knew that she must have hands because someone was holding them gently, urging her to rise to the surface. And there was a steadily growing light, too, a soft glow at the end of this sloping tunnel. Still distant, she heard a woman's voice quite clearly.

'Oh! Gott sei Dank—Master, her eyelids, they are flickering!'

It was a safe, kind voice—one that she trusted but could not quite remember. Then: 'Eloise! My dearest heart—wake up.' The command was tender and yearning, yet there was urgency in it too and she wanted to obey. With a supreme effort she opened her eyes for a second and saw the dear face, haggard with anxiety, close to her own.

'Anton?' she whispered thickly, but her eyelids were too heavy and quickly drooped again. But she was aware of deep, deep happiness and the last of the darkness melted away—she was *alive*.

Another man's voice, older, crisper, said: 'At last—I think she will do, now,' and, although the strong, dear hands went on holding hers more firmly, new, bony fingers closed round her wrist and her eyes flew open without effort, filled with fear.

'My darling—don't be afraid,' Anton said softly. 'It is only Dr Arst, who is feeling your pulse. There is no danger, nor ever will be again.'

'I thought ...' she began weakly, but speaking was too difficult. Instead she looked round her and, as slow recognition dawned, she tried to smile. She was lying in a deep, soft bed with shaded candles keeping the full light from her eyes. Beside her knelt Anton, his dark eyes smiling encouragingly into hers, while just beyond, tears streaming down her face, stood Frau Schnelling. Eloise hadn't the strength to turn her head towards the doctor. With a little sigh of content-ment she closed her eyes again and drifted off into a quiet, healing sleep.

For three days Eloise had lain unconscious after Anton brought her back to the house in Josefstrasse, sending for the finest physicians while he and Frau Schnelling kept endless vigil by her bedside. Miracul-ously, von Eckerman's murderous thrust had gone wide of her heart but caused a deep flesh wound in her side, and she had lost much blood. This had been stitched and bandaged by a surgeon, experienced in treating duelling wounds, who had been briefly called by Dr Arnst. For the rest, Anton's heart ached as the doctor, helped by Frau Schnelling, cleaned and applied soothing balms and ointments to all her sligh-ter wounds—the cruel cuts and grazes, the livid bruises and her twisted ankle, that was so swollen that Frau Schnelling applied poultices every few hours.

'You should get rest,' Dr Arst said to him firmly. 'You too have been wounded, and undergone a great ordeal into the bargain, I gather.'

'I refuse to leave her side, even for an hour,' Anton replied with equal firmness. 'I alone am to blame for her terrible plight—what right have I to rest?'

The doctor shrugged—it was useless to argue.

Anton sent one footman to fetch his lawyer, and another to bring the manager of his stables to the house—even so, he only saw them briefly just outside Eloise's door. He ordered his lawyer to purchase the phaeton that had caused Eloise so much fear and have it destroyed, also to see to a private burial for von Eckerman out in the country. He heard, with relief, that thanks to his long, agonisingly slow progress down from Semmering, carrying Eloise, Leo had suffered no serious ill effects.

But it was to be six days after her first signs of consciousness before Dr Arst would allow Eloise to be propped up on pillows and talk for a little while. Tactfully, he and Frau Schnelling withdrew, leaving her alone with Anton.

'Oh, I am so truly sorry,' she began swiftly, her huge eyes entreating him to understand. 'I have been so much trouble, and now have become a burden again.'

'Sorry? A burden—*you*?' he exclaimed passionately. 'My most beloved one, *I* am the one to be sorry! If you had died I believe I should have killed myself. It took your note, the terrible knowledge that you were in danger, to bring me to my senses and let me accept the truth: that I have loved you with all my heart and soul, ever since I saw you. That *you* are the great and only love of my life, beloved Eloise, and the girl I thought I loved when I was twenty was no more than a shadow—a boyish dream that never really existed in truth at all! My darling—can you ever forgive me? I dare not ask if you can love me, for ...'

She put tender fingers over his lips, her eyes glowing dark purple now. 'Anton, *don't*—you are the whole world to me and I know that you acted from pure nobility, my darling,' she smiled. 'Don't ever *dare* to demean yourself to me!'

Years fell away from his face and his eyes glowed like her own. 'After all that has happened—you mean you will really consider being my wife?' he asked, almost in awe. 'Oh, Eloise—what in all my selfish life, warped and fiercely guarded against all emotions because I refused to grow up, have I done to deserve you?'

'Waited for me—without knowing it. Had I finally lost you, my life would have been a sad, empty thing. I think deep in my heart there was hope, even when I ran away. To be your wife will be all happiness, all fulfilment ...'

She could say no more, for he had gently gathered her up in his arms as she spoke, careful not to hurt her wounds, and his mouth claimed hers with such exquisite tenderness and consideration that she knew a bliss beyond her wildest dreams.

When, at last, he rested her back against the pillows, his hands close over hers, she said: 'I have known for some days that I am lying in your beautiful East Wing, Anton, but—where is the portrait?' Her eyes turned to the empty wall between the tall windows.

'Gone—like the shade she was. I sent it back to her

father, who gave it to me, days ago.' There was such a youthful joyousness and release in his voice that her last doubts were laid to rest. 'She never saw this East Wing,' he went on eagerly. 'It was designed and decorated by me as a bridal suite—designed from my dreams of what love should be, not knowing that my *real* great love was still a little girl at the time!' he added with a charming smile, mocking himself.

'Do you want to tell me about her? The girl in the portrait?'

His brow creased in genuine bewilderment: 'Do you know, my darling, I can scarcely remember her? It seems incredible now that a lively young music student in Salzburg captured my imagination so completely with a few kisses that I actually turned this into a shrine for her. That when I found she was flagrantly unfaithful the moment I left Salzburg for Vienna, when my father died and I inherited his titles and estates so that there was much to settle—taking many months—I judged all women by her perfidy? I lived a monastic life here during that time—preparing this East Wing, believing she would marry me—only to return unexpectedly to claim her and find her in the embrace of another man!'

Eloise released her hands and lifted them protectively to his face. 'Anton—you, of all people! How could she?'

'Because—lovely as she was, though not half as beautiful as you—she had no heart. No heart at all. So I decided that no woman on earth could be trusted.' His face darkened a little. 'I have punished many women since for her shallowness,' he said seriously, then lifted his eyes to meet hers. 'I earned my title "Count Satan"—you have to believe that, my darling, and know whether your love is generous enough to accept it, for it is true.'

'Never for me—it never has been,' she cried. 'When you first came across the room to meet me my only impression was of sadness—a sadness I have prayed ever since that I might be able to lift.' Then she went on, her eyes clouding: 'But we must talk about Gerhard—I try with all my might to forget him but I cannot, and there is much I must explain.'

'You have nothing to explain at all, my love. He was born an out and out rogue and a creature also without a heart. You heard his confession, saw the cards with which he cheated us all to make his living. Being charming to women was part of his game, since he knew that men distrusted him and seldom invited him to their homes—but women asked him to escort them and so he gained entry to all the finest houses. Then he met you. . . .'

Anton relinquished her hands and got up, pacing up and down beside the bed for a few minutes as he wrestled with his innate honesty, his hatred of von Eckerman and yet the deep debt he owed to him. Eloise watched him quietly, saying nothing.

At last: 'I think, in his corrupt way, he probably loved you, Eloise.' It was an admission that pained him, but he felt it to be true—and it would surely help her to lay her fears to rest. 'Only he had no means of winning you by fair means and so—as always—he resorted to trickery.'

He returned to the chair by her bed and his dark eyes met hers squarely. 'I believe—and I pray that you will believe it too—that out there on the mountain he had run quite mad, or he would never have tried to hurt you. And in spite of all his dishonesty, I owe him more than life itself for forcing me to face the truth and bringing us together again. Can you—possibly—try to think of him in that light, my love?'

She turned her head to the window for a while, thinking seriously about this new prospect of the man who had abused and frightened her beyond all endurance. Then slowly the memory of his cruel hands, his lustful kisses and the livid, rain-drenched face pursuing her through the storm began to fade. Instead she found herself remembering the tall, fair man who had been such a gracious partner at balls, who had gone out of his way to be her friend, and at last horror gave way to sorrowful, healing pity.

She turned back to Anton, who was watching her anxiously, with a radiant smile, although her face was pale.

'My darling—thank you. You have exorcised the fear, and I think I shall never dream of that terrible night again.'

He leant forward and kissed her as he said: 'No—all that has gone for ever, and there are so many wonderful dreams of the future waiting for you, beloved ... for now you must rest.'

Three months later they were married in the magnificent Stefanskirche, the great building packed with all Viennese society gathered to wish them well. But humbler friends had places of honour, too: Frau Schnelling, weeping copious tears of joy, in the fine green velvet dress Eloise had had made for her; Dr Arnst in his professional black but sporting fine white ruffles in honour of the occasion. The manager of

Anton's stables representing Leo, who should—as
Eloise had said earlier—have been Guest of Honour,
and even the young footman from the von Holst house
who had carried her note to Josefstrasse on the night
before she ran away. The Gräfin and her two
daughters concealed jealously behind a smirk. But to
Anton's delight, Eloise had invited Graf von Holst to
give her away.

Before the ceremony began she stood in the porch
with that kindly, wise old man, and his eyes moist as he
looked at her. Her great beauty was incandescent in a
white satin gown embroidered all over with delicate
silver leaves and clusters of sparkling rhinestones
forming little flowers, her veil held in place by the
diamond coronet of the von Arnheims. Beyond all the
sleek heads of men and puffed hair and chic hats of
women, she could see Anton waiting for her, so tall
and handsome in white knee-breeches and a coat of
turquoise satin embossed with silver. Impulsively she
turned to the Graf and kissed his cheek.

'I wish I had listened to your wisdom earlier,' she
said. 'Yet if I had this day of miracles might never have
happened! But I will always listen to you in future, I
promise.'

He patted her white-gloved hand on his arm.

'My dear, you will not need to—you are marrying a
man in a million. Come—we must not keep him waiting.'

Anton and Eloise had let it be known to all their
friends that they planned to honeymoon in
France—only the staff in Josefstrasse, under strict
oath of secrecy, had to be told their real intention. So,
when the reception had lasted for some four hours,

they went upstairs with due ceremony to change for the long drive.

Frau Schnelling was waiting for Eloise in her old room, giggling a little after two glasses of champagne and also because their idea appealed to her deeply hidden romantic streak.

'Everything is ready, Countess,' she said with a little bobbed curtsey. But Eloise drew her to her feet and hugged her.

'Has any woman—ever—been so happy?' she cried, her face glowing. 'Now help me, for I can scarce bear my dear husband out of my sight!'

She slipped out of the wedding gown and Frau Schnelling helped her into an elegant travelling outfit of cream gabardine with a bodice of ruffled lace and a close-fitting little jacket which did full justice to her slight, graceful figure.

When she was ready she found Anton, also changed, waiting for her in the passage. She ran into his arms and together they laughed joyously as they kissed—then, with mock solemnity, he drew her hand through his arm and said: 'Now for the charade, my darling—oh, I can scarce wait to have you to myself!'

As they walked down the stairs a sea of faces looked up and cheered, calling good wishes and throwing single flowers. Outside the carriage, duly decked with ribbons and flowers, was waiting, and Anton handed her in with grave solemnity and the driver, grinning with pleasure, flicked the horses and they were off . . . but not towards the road that eventually led to Paris. Instead, through a carefully planned route, they came to the stables where the main gates stood open so that the carriage could drive right in.

Leaving the driver and some of the stable lads to

remove all the wedding decorations, Anton and
Eloise went on to Leo's stall. Within half an hour
darkness had fallen and the bridal pair re-entered
their carriage and were driven by another circuitous
route to the back entrance of the house in Josefstrasse, in case a few guests were still lingering and
celebrating.

They went in hand in hand, and as they crossed the
kitchen all the staff stood, smiling, and raised their
tankards. Then they went up the back stairs and along
to where Frau Schnelling was waiting to help Eloise
undress—still in her old room, using it for the last
time. A selection of hand-embroidered nightgowns
and bed-robes were laid out on the bed for Eloise to
make her selection from this exquisite trousseau. But
she shook her head, her eyes shining.

'No, Frau Schnelling. Tomorrow I will use one, but
for tonight I shall go to my husband in my own, pale
yellow robe.'

Frau Schnelling threw up her hands, about to protest—for this, the wealthiest bride in Vienna, to go to
her bridal in a simple country robe was unthinkable.
But when she saw the secret smile hovering round
Eloise's mouth she said nothing, and soon she slipped
quietly away, leaving Eloise sitting by the fire waiting
for her husband. Briefly she remembered the hours of
bitterness and sorrow spent in that very chair—but
her heart was so filled with joy that quickly, like
Gerhard von Eckerman, they faded gently into the
past.

'Eloise!'

She had not heard him open the door and sprang up
to face him, her cheeks becomingly flushed with
sudden modesty. Then he strode forward and swept

her up into his arms, murmuring: 'My little love—my wife—did you know that I was hoping you would wear that very robe? It has played a large part in our lives, my darling,' and he kissed her. Her arms slid round his neck and, with her lovely head on his shoulder, he carried her along the passage and into the East Wing, beautifully lit and ablaze with flowers.

'Oh, Anton—at last we have truly come home!' And she raised her face to his.

Masquerade
Historical Romances

Intrigue
excitement
romance

Don't miss
September's
other enthralling Historical Romance title

CROMWELL'S CAPTAIN
by Anne Madden

Why does Cathie Gifford, who comes of a staunchly
Royalist family, feel compelled to tend the wounded
Roundhead captain she finds lying in the grounds of
their Devon estate? For Piers Denham, a handsome
aristocrat, has chosen to fight against his own kind
and serve as a captain under Cromwell. Doubly an
enemy, he is now at the mercy of Cathie and her
beautiful widowed cousin Rachel, who has fled from
Exeter to seek refuge with the Giffords.

Why should such a man cause Cathie to doubt her
loyalty to the King's cause? And why should she
resent so fiercely the fact that Rachel Devereux seems
more welcome at Piers' bedside than Cathie herself?

You can obtain this title today from your local paperback
retailer

Masquerade
Historical Romances

Intrigue excitement romance

TARRISBROKE HALL
by Jasmine Cresswell

Utter ruin confronted the Earl of Tarrisbroke. Faced
with discharging his father's mountainous gambling
debts, what could he do but marry for money? But
the wife he chose, the wealthy young widow Marianne
Johnson, was not at all the vulgar title-hunting woman
he expected!

ZULU SUNSET
by Christina Laffeaty

Cassandra Hudson wanted to be a missionary's wife
— more particularly, her cousin Martin's wife. So she
travelled to Zululand to visit him, confident that her
new fortune would smooth her way. Unfortunately
she found herself in the midst of an impending war
between whites and Zulus, and the only man who
could help her reach Martin was the odious, arrogant
Saul Parnell . . .

Look out for these titles in your local paperback shop from
10th October 1980

Doctor Nurse Romances

and September's
stories of romantic relationships behind the scenes
of modern medical life are:

FIRST YEAR LOVE
by Clare Lavenham

When Kate started her nursing career at Northleigh
Hospital, she was thrilled to recognise the consultant
surgeon as a long-time friend of her brother's. Might her
childish hero-worship now blossom into something more
mature? Or was she looking in the wrong direction
altogether?

SURGEON IN CHARGE
(Winter of Change)
by Betty Neels

Mary Jane was over twenty-one, and a competent staff
nurse, so when she inherited a fortune she was furious
to find that she also had a guardian — the high-handed
Fabian van der Blocq. But what could she do about it
— or him?

Order your copies today from your local paperback retailer

Masquerade
Historical Romances

Intrigue excitement romance

MEETING AT SCUTARI
by Belinda Grey

Even Jessica Linton, bored with the triviality of
Victorian society, was not prepared to flout convention
by having an affair with a married man. So, to forget
her love for Prince Paul Varinsky, she embarked for
Scutari in the Crimea, as one of Florence Nightingale's
staff, and found herself with the army that was fighting
Paul's countrymen . . .

THE DEVIL'S ANGEL
by Ann Edgeworth

Why should Mistress Prue Angel seem so reluctant to
encourage the handsome, rakish Duke of Carlington
after chance throws them together? The Duke was
certainly known throughout Georgian London as the
Perfidious Devil, and renowned for his *amours,* but
could an unknown like Prue afford to spurn his
advances?

These titles are still available through your local paperback
retailer